'How perfectly awful for you!'

Ross read her eyes clearly. Of all things, Gina had decided to be sorry for him. 'It happens,' he snapped. 'I'm not the first and I shan't be the last to have to dust myself down and start again.'

'I'm sure all of us will do our very best to help in any way we can,' she said at once, undeterred, her eyes soft, their earlier encounter apparently non-existent.

He wasn't going to forget it, though. He was not going to be patronised by anyone, spinal injuries or not, least of all by this know-all with her out-of-control Jag. 'I am planning to stand on my own two feet,' he informed her icily.

Dear Reader

We're only travelling far with one book this month, as Lilian Darcy takes us cruising Bermudan waters in RUNNING AWAY. A MAN OF HONOUR by Caroline Anderson is a deeply moving book, while Jean Evans gives us her first vet book set on Jersey with THE FRAGILE HEART. Elizabeth Harrison gives us a hero with spinal injuries in THE SENIOR PARTNER'S DAUGHTER, all of which makes up a perfectly super month. Do enjoy!

The Editor

After several years as a medical secretary in London hospitals and in general practice, **Elizabeth Harrison** went to a voluntary medical organisation as associate editor. Here she was also responsible for arranging programmes in the UK for postgraduate doctors and nurses from overseas. She enjoys pottering about in boats, cooking in a slapdash way and trying to keep up with her garden overlooking Richmond Park. She is a Vice-President of the Romantic Novelists' Association.

Recent titles by the same author:

THE FAITHFUL TYPE
THE SURGEON SHE MARRIED

THE SENIOR PARTNER'S DAUGHTER

BY

ELIZABETH HARRISON

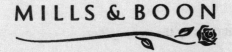

MILLS & BOON

MILLS & BOON LIMITED
ETON HOUSE, 18–24 PARADISE ROAD
RICHMOND, SURREY, TW9 1SR

*First published in Great Britain 1994
by Mills & Boon Limited*

© Elizabeth Harrison 1994

*Australian copyright 1994   Philippine copyright 1994
This edition 1994*

ISBN 0 263 78593 9

*Set in 10 on 11½ pt Linotron Times
03-9405-55713*

*Typeset in Great Britain by Centracet, Cambridge
Made and printed in Great Britain*

CHAPTER ONE

MRS WINTER came to the gate with Gina, and saw her into the car tenderly, though she was still grey with worry. 'You're absolutely right,' she said. 'And I'm so grateful. She'll be better off in the ward.'

'I do honestly think so. Only for a day or two, after all. Until she's over this particular infection.'

Mrs Winter nodded. 'I'll see you later, then, in Vicky's. Thank you ever so much for coming out, Doctor, and for taking all this trouble.'

'Until this evening, then,' Gina said, and drove away with a quick wave. She was going to be late, but the delay had been worthwhile. She'd not only examined Susie thoroughly, but had a really good talk to her and to her mother. It was, after all, for this sort of opportunity she'd left Mortimer's, her teaching hospital in London, and returned to her home town of Northborough to join her father's general practice. George Hurst was in his sixties, and he had a heart problem, but his health had not been her only reason for coming home. She hadn't liked what was happening to her at Mortimer's. It had been as simple as that.

She'd loved the challenge, of course, and she knew she was going to miss the stimulus of working alongside the top minds in her field of general medicine. But she had begun to hate the way she spent her days and the person she seemed to be turning into. The pace and the inescapable fatigue were changing her — for the worse, she felt — while what had once been the invigorating anticipation of the day ahead had turned into the ordeal of a never-ending hassle. Once she had welcomed each new chance to look after another human being up against it. She'd longed to greet new patients, to be able to look for the cause of their symptoms and diagnose their condition, and then watch them set out on the road to recovery. No longer, though. Now she was tired to the bone, and each morning had brought her simply a stolid determination to survive the next twenty-four hours without actually letting anyone down.

She'd felt she was becoming an automaton. An uncaring automaton, wanting only to be shot of one problem so that she could be away fast to the next on the list.

This wasn't what had taken her into medicine. People and a longing to be able to help them had been what motivated her then. But at Mortimer's there turned out to be no time for human beings. Only cases. Interesting cases. Day after day.

Here in Northborough, though, there was time to talk to people, to follow them into their homes, find out how they lived, and how treating their illness could be carried on against the normal background of their everyday existence.

Which was what she had just been doing at the Winters'. Susie Winter was sixteen, and she had cystic fibrosis. As a result of this, her damaged lungs were at the mercy of every chance infection—yet another of which she'd just picked up. Gina wanted to pop her straight into Vicky's—more correctly known as Queen Victoria's Hospital, Northborough.

Both Susie and her mother had resisted this plan at first, insisting that they could manage perfectly well at home, but Gina had finally succeeded in talking them round. It had taken time, though, and patience—and understanding, too, though of this she was hardly aware. And now she was, as so often, running late.

She slowed the powerful Jag—her pride and joy, this at least one of the bonus points of leaving London, together with her flat with its huge mortgage—and turned off the bypass. She'd save a few minutes by cutting through the lanes, avoiding the traffic jams that built up over the lunch hour at the roundabout.

She had a busy afternoon ahead. She had to grab some lunch before the well baby clinic, which was to be followed by the interview with the new assistant her father had somehow managed to drum up from his own teaching hospital. Then there'd still be half her visits to fit in before evening surgery, and after that Susie to see again, this time in Vicky's.

However, it wasn't quite one-thirty. There was really no need for all this rush and tear and split-second timing. It was a habit, left over from her days at Mortimer's. This is Northborough, not London, she reminded herself. Calm down. Slow down, too. No need to drive as if you're testing the car at Brooklands.

It was fun, though. She loved driving this powerful machine of hers, and there was hardly ever any traffic on this narrow lane winding its way over the downs. No one used it except farm workers and the odd milk lorry. She pushed the revs up, driving at the margin of her skill and loving every minute, slowing into each bend and accelerating out of it as if she were rallying. Only this last double bend, and then the straight when the lane widened, and she'd be nearly home.

She tore into the final bend, enjoying every second, and hurtled out of it. And jammed on her brakes, changing down, gripping the wheel as she assessed her exact chances, regaining control almost before she lost it, and coming to a juddering halt with the Jag's nose in the high hedge and the nearside wheel no more than millimetres from the rear bumper of an ancient Ford that ought by rights, she thought furiously, to have been sent to the dump.

She discovered she'd been holding her breath, let it out thankfully, and refilled her lungs ready to inform the Ford's owner what she thought of him, his car, its roadworthiness — was there even the faintest chance it had passed its MOT? — and his road sense.

Big, broad-shouldered, he was slow to move. Some farm labourer, clearly, used to taking his time, moving ponderously, with a mind as deliberate as his movements, no doubt.

However, he beat her to the draw.

'What,' he enquired in a biting, incisive tone that was not in the least what she had been expecting, 'do you imagine you're doing, rocketing round the corner like a maniac?'

His voice was not rural, either. Clipped and commanding, rather, reminiscent of overbearing consultants at their nastiest, demolishing unfortunate juniors on teaching rounds.

'And what,' Gina came back at him fast, 'what, one wonders, do you imagine you're doing, parking this — this *object* on a narrow bend?' Her words might have been offensive — they were certainly intended to be — but her voice was silky-smooth.

He was standing where he had been when she first caught sight of him, between the car and the hedge. 'Lucky for me,' he pointed out, 'that I'd the car to screen me from that lethal weapon you're operating so dangerously.' He followed this comment by walking cautiously round the decrepit old heap and settling himself firmly, his narrow hips resting negligently against the bonnet while he searched the pockets of the shabby anorak he wore above faded denim for what turned out, when he discovered them, to be a notebook and ballpoint. This he clicked, and then proceeded to write something down, squinting sideways at the Jag before doing so

He was taking her number. Who did he think he was?

Her fury redoubled. 'I'd be obliged if you'd move your machine,' she said between gritted teeth. 'I'd like to get by.'

'No doubt. But it's not on.'

'I *beg* your pardon?'

He had the effrontery to chuckle. 'Oh, no, you don't you know.'

Gina swallowed. She was not going to lose her cool, but holding on was difficult, and getting more so with every syllable he uttered. 'I have an appointment,' she announced in clear, carrying tones as authoritative as she could make them. 'I need you to move your vehicle so that I can get past.'

'Sorry. Nothing doing.'

Not only was he unapologetic, he seemed to be enjoying the situation.

Gina climbed out of the Jag. 'What did you say?'

She was standing over him, he supposed, in an attempt to bully him. 'Nothing doing,' he repeated. He looked her up and down, dislike clearly visible. Obviously he detested her and everything she stood for—probably he resented the fact that she, a woman, was driving the powerful Jag while he had only his old heap.

She was only partly right. At first, Ross Nicholson had assumed her to be the spoilt young daughter of some wealthy local tycoon, joy-riding in her father's car, irresponsible and out of hand. He was revising this first impression, though. She might well be spoilt, and no doubt she was also someone's daughter. But she was also, he guessed, a power-hungry woman executive in her own right, clad in the executive's pinstripe, pristine white shirt fastened high at the neck. Lacquered from the top of her shining dark head to the toes of her equally shining black shoes, she wore pearls and a small gold pin. Both real, for sure. No doubt her briefcase, Filofax and portable telephone, with her lap-top computer, accompanied her everywhere.

'Look,' she was saying, 'as I told you, I have an appointment. I need your car moved.' Her tone was icy now, her eyes green, and venomous.

'Afraid you're going to be out of luck. You'll have to go back the way you came,' he told her, and for good measure shrugged the broad shoulders, though otherwise he'd not moved from his relaxed position, propped up by his rusting apology for a car.

Gina said nothing whatever. She was counting up to ten, knowing that to unclench her teeth and open her mouth would have meant an explosion. She was not going to allow herself to stand in any country lane screaming hysterically at some yob.

Her silence had some effect, for at least the Ford's owner at last went so far as to proffer an explanation.

'Out of petrol,' he said crisply.

Gina could see, though, that inwardly he was amused at her predicament. His dark eyes, that throughout their exchange had held a suppressed amusement, gleamed with laughter he was hardly bothering any longer to conceal. He was a male chauvinist who thought her of no account, just another silly woman fussed about time-keeping.

'You can push it, can't you?' she was brusque.

He shook his head. 'No.'

What did he mean? He was playing games with her, needling her, refusing to co-operate in any way, waiting to see whether she lost her temper or burst into tears. Then he'd have won. Well, he wasn't going to win. And she wasn't going to back down the lane the way she'd come.

She strolled across the lane and assessed the lie of the land, her movements long-legged and as assertive as she could make them. 'Before I can back,' she commented affably, 'we'll need your vehicle about a foot or eighteen inches forward. That wouldn't seem to present too much of a problem.'

In a somewhat ungainly fashion—perhaps she'd at last succeeded in getting under his skin—he heaved himself off the Ford's bonnet. 'Go ahead,' he agreed amiably. 'If you're set on it.'

He took her breath away, but she set her lips and made a determined effort to wipe her face clean of all expression, to present him with a blank front. If that was how he was going to be, she could deal with it. She was, surely, capable of pushing his disgusting pile of junk twelve miserable inches forward? He could stand there and watch, and see how he liked that.

But again he beat her to it.

He opened the Ford's door, settled himself cosily in the driving seat. 'Let me know when you're ready,' he offered sunnily. 'I'll release the hand brake as soon as you say.'

He was enjoying himself. The dark eyes were bright with amusement still. He was waiting to see how far she'd go, at what stage she'd give in and back down. Well, he'd find out. Stony-faced, Gina stepped round the car on the grass bank by the hedge, positioned herself behind it, scuffed her feet until she was sure of her foothold, established her hand hold, and called, 'Right. Ready when you are,' as coolly as she knew how.

'Brake off,' came the prompt reply.

Gina pushed. The Ford remained stationary. She pushed harder. Nothing happened. She took a deep breath, put her back into it. She wasn't, couldn't be, going to fail. Impossible. Unthinkable.

The car moved forward, and suddenly it was easy. The Ford was rolling. She could push it for ever.

She'd won.

She strolled through the space she'd made between the two cars, glanced along the lane ahead of them. 'You know,' she said airily, 'if you'd steer a bit more to the near side, and I give you another shove, I could get round you. No need to reverse. Then I might not be late for my appointment after all.'

'By all means,' he said. His jaw was jutting, and she noticed with considerable pleasure that now he spoke between gritted teeth, and the humour had entirely left his long, narrow face.

'The Cross Keys is the nearest garage,' she informed him kindly. 'Would you like me to call in and ask them to come out and rescue you?' Her lip curled triumphantly.

'Not necessary, thank you so much.' It was his turn for the velvet touch. 'My companion should have reached there by now, so I'll wait for him, and in the meanwhile trust that no other maniac takes the bend at seventy.'

She turned on her heel—her somewhat dusty heel, she registered as she stepped back into the Jag— reversed out of the hedge, crept carefully round the Ford and its occupant with a nonchalant wave and a gracious smile, and drove off along the lane.

Half a mile further along, she passed a tall figure swinging along towards her and carrying a can of petrol. So that was that. All over and done with.

Or so she thought.

Two hours later, Andy Forsyth, the tall figure who'd been carrying the petrol, drove his battered Ford into the gravel sweep in front of a vast red-brick Victorian house. There were four cars already parked there—a Bentley, a Mercedes, a Citroën, and a Jaguar. 'A wealthy up-market practice,' he commented.

'You're more right than you realise,' his passenger Ross Nicholson, told him. 'I simply don't believe it. Except that I do.' He dived into an inner pocket—he had changed out of the anorak and denim, and was very formally attired in a dark suit, striped shirt and a Central London Hospital tie—produced his notebook and riffled through its pages. 'Yes,' he said grimly. 'Exactly as I suspected. No mistake. That Jag, would you believe, is the vehicle with whose charming driver I had my confrontation while you were getting the petrol.'

Andy's jaw dropped. 'You don't mean it. It can't be.'

'Oh, yes, it can. That Jag belongs to that bossy woman in her pinstripe. Of course, she could be a patient, but the chances are she's one of the partners about to give me the once-over.'

'But I thought the job was more or less fixed. I thought Leo and the senior partner had it lined up for you.'

'That's right. I just had to show up this afternoon, be introduced to the other partners over a cup of tea, and bingo, I'd be in. But madam may have something to say about that.'

'If it comes to that, you may have something to say yourself. I mean, do you want the post, if it means working with that incredible female? We could just pack it in — I can drive you straight back to town, and you can simply forget about it. Leo would understand.'

'Oh, I think I'll give it a whirl, you know. Might be quite interesting. Anyway, I can't just duck the appointment.'

'I'll wait for you, anyway. Then, if it comes to nothing, I'll drive you straight back to the Rose and Crown, we can cancel your booking, collect your bag, and be off.'

'No, you go straight back as we'd planned. I'm supposed to be having dinner with the senior partner, in any case. Can't duck that either — don't want to, in fact. After all, George Hurst came up to the Central especially to see me and talk over my problems and his job. No, if it remains an offer, I'm taking the job. If madam likes to apply the veto, that's up to her. It's four o'clock. I'd better go in. Don't wait, Andy, it's not necessary. Get back to town for your evening date.' Ross levered himself out of the aged Ford's sagging seat, crunched across the well-raked gravel, climbed the shallow steps to the porch, and stopped before four highly polished brass plates. The top one bore the name of the partner he'd already met, Dr G. M. D. Hurst, MD, MRCP, DCH. The second said Dr J. R. Black, the third Dr A. M. Patel, and the fourth — this was going to be more complicated than he'd supposed — the fourth read Dr Georgina Hurst, MD, MRCP. That opinionated chit appeared to be the daughter of the delightful George Hurst. She was well qualified, too. Ross's mouth quirked. The introduction to the partners, which had seemed so straightforward, if not almost dull, when he'd set off that morning, now looked more like a potential battleground, and he experienced that unmistakable *frisson* of excitement that went with an imminent challenge. The afternoon promised fireworks rather than boredom, and his eyes held the sparks that Gina would have recognised.

He rang the bell.

A cheerful-looking woman with crisp greying curls let him in, greeted him pleasantly, saying he was expected, and led him across a wide hall into a large bay-windowed room overlooking a garden brilliant with daffodils swaying in the March wind.

Four faces turned towards Ross. One of them dropped about a foot, he was pleased to notice, his own expression bland and impenetrable.

The next hour, though, was to prove more than difficult, and in a way he had not foreseen, though it began painlessly enough, with routine introductions made by George Hurst. The two unknown faces turned out to belong to James Black, a tall Scot with fair, untidy hair and a long, humorous face, and Amrit Patel, a quietly beautiful Indian woman wearing a very British tweed skirt with a soft cashmere sweater. The fourth member of the party George Hurst, as Ross had expected, introduced as his daughter.

'We have, in fact, already met,' Ross responded. 'Isn't that so?' His voice was neutral and gave nothing away.

'Indeed.' The reply was curt, but Gina Hurst added nothing to the two brief syllables.

George Hurst gave his daughter a mildly puzzled glance, but almost immediately the receptionist returned with a tray of tea, and was herself introduced as Betty Armstrong. She distributed tea and biscuits, and then departed, and Ross's ordeal began.

It was not an ordeal by fire, but rather by acute

embarrassment, which he'd not anticipated, though it began easily enough.

'Sorry to see Leo hasn't been able to make it this afternoon, after all,' George said.

'No. He had this summons to Brussels to some VIP whose hernia popped out, so he had to take off *stat*, and leave me to make my own way down.' Leo Rosenstein, senior surgeon at the Central London Hospital, had once been George Hurst's chief, and it was Leo who had recommended Ross for the post on offer — if, of course, it was still on offer. That remained to be seen. 'He sends his apologies.'

'Sorry not to see him today, of course, but no matter,' George assured him. 'I think I know enough about your past career and your present problems to be able to stand in for him at this stage.'

And so the ordeal began. As Ross tried to present a succinct account of his medical career — in fact originally a surgical career — George constantly interruped and supplemented everything with his own glowing additions. Ross learned that he was the most outstanding house surgeon and then registrar Leo Rosenstein had had in twenty years at the Central, that in his later appointments he had shown brilliance and dedication, and that, in short, hospitals all over the country, if not the world, maybe the universe, were savagely competing for the privilege of employing him.

Ross kept trying to tone it down, bring it back into the realms of ordinary everyday existence. He had no success whatever.

At last, they reached his current appointment at the Central, his mundane post as a clinical manager.

James Black was puzzled. 'You've left surgery for the management sphere?' he enquired, frowning.

'Surgery has left me,' Ross said quickly. 'I was in a car crash, and ——'

George took over again. 'He had spinal injuries, and spent two years in Stoke Mandeville on his back. Isn't that right?'

'More or less.' Ross gave up trying to stop George in his tracks. Entirely due to his well-meant enthusiasm, Ross was letting the interview get away from him, he realised uneasily.

'Two years in Stoke,' George ploughed inexorably on. 'Another year in the Central's rehabilitation unit, and another year getting back to work in management, right? So a period in general practice would be the next stage of rehabilitation, eh?'

'That's right. If you all feel inclined to take me on,' Ross said. Engrossed in his damage-limitation exercise with George, he had not been watching Gina. She had been watching him, though, her green eyes widening, and now she exploded into speech.

'You had spinal injuries, and you aren't going to be fit for surgery any longer?' she asked.

Ross turned his head sharply. What was she getting at? That if he wasn't fit for surgery he certainly wasn't fit for general practice? 'That's correct,' he responded crisply.

Her next comment was almost the exact opposite to what he had been expecting. 'That's absolutely terrible!' she said poignantly. 'How perfectly awful for you.'

Her eyes were filled with pain and compassion. Ross read them clearly. Of all things, she had decided to be sorry for him. This he was not going to wear. No way. 'It happens,' he snapped. 'As an accident surgeon, I've seen it again and again. I'm not the first and I shan't be the last to have to dust myself down and start again.' He was hurling his words across the room at her.

'I'm sure all of us will do our very best to help in any way we can,' she said at once, undeterrred, her eyes soft, their earlier encounter apparently non-existent.

He wasn't going to forget it, though. He was not going to be patronised by anyone, spinal injuries or not, least of all by this know-all with her out-of-control Jag. 'I am planning to stand on my own two feet,' he informed her icily. 'Which thankfully I'm now able to do, even if not for hours on end. What I'm here to discuss is whether the hours I can work will meet the needs of this practice. I do have to say frankly that my services are bound to be limited by a necessity for more rest periods during the day than is normal.' There it was. At any rate he'd taken the interview back into his own hands again.

James Black had watched, and sympathised with, Ross's unease when George was hyping him up, and he understood at once why, on top of that, Gina's sympathy might have little appeal. He wouldn't have cared for any of it himself. Both the Hursts were overdoing it. Time for him to step in. From now on, he was going to run this discussion, not George. And certainly not Gina.

'Tell me,' he said, addressing Ross directly, 'approximately how long you are able to stand without a rest period?'

Thankful to be asked a straight question at last, Ross tried to give an equally straight answer. 'You've put your finger on my main problem, which is that I can't exactly tell. I can still get very occasional bouts of postural hypotension, when I have to sit down fast before I pass out.'

'Awkward,' James said, somewhat drily.

'Exactly. The verdict at the Central is that the nerves of the spinal cord are still somewhat confused about their new pathways, and every so often get their messages misrouted. The neurologists' opinion is that these episodes will almost certainly get fewer, and should eventually cease altogether. No one can find anything amiss with my heart and circulation — and don't think the cardiologists haven't tried. I've had every test known to man.'

'You do have quite a problem there,' James said slowly. 'And not only for yourself. For all of us, if you begin work here.'

'Exactly. And that's why I shall quite understand if you feel you can't take me on.' Ross was downright. 'OK, so I'm comparatively highly qualified clinically for an assistant in general practice, as George has been pointing out. But that isn't going to help anyone if I'm going to be out of action when I'm needed. And I do think that's the crux of it.'

George stepped in, a bit emotionally, to point out that Ross's qualifications and past experience far out-weighed those of any other candidate they'd seen. 'If you think that doesn't count, then I despair. I suppose the next thing will be you'll want to boot me out, because my heart may become a liability to the prac-tice,' he ended, his face flushed.

James Black, evidently used to his senior partner, panicked not at all. He smiled affectionately across at George and said, 'Come off it, you old terror. You know that's a non-starter.'

'Perhaps I was a bit over the top,' George admitted, calming down at once. 'Got a bit excited again, I'm afraid. Sorry.'

'All the same,' Gina put in with feeling, 'it does

seem to me there's a good deal in what Dad said.
We're supposed to be doctors, aren't we, here to care
for the sick? If we can't begin to look after one of our
own colleagues when they need help, what *are* we
coming to?'

'I don't need any looking after, thank you very
much,' Ross retorted instantly—and unwisely, he
recognised as soon as he'd spoken.

James Black was smiling at him, only too evidently
reading his mind. 'I think, maybe, you do a little,' he
suggested peaceably.

'Sorry. Yes, of course I do. Moreover, it's what
we're here to discuss, the amount of help I need, and
how much use I can be in spite of that.' He took a
deep breath. 'So back to the problem of how long I
can stand without a rest of some sort—without sitting
down, is what it amounts to. As long as I'm not
standing non-stop, I can carry on as long as anyone
else. The trouble is that at present these hypotensive
episodes do seem to come right out of the blue—or
they do as far as I'm concerned. I have no warning. At
the Central, I'm bound to say, they usually spotted the
onset before I did—well, I change colour, of course,
and sweat—and they'd go into action, interrupt me,
make me lie down and raise my legs, no matter where
we happened to be. Embarrassing but effective. But
I've got to learn to cope with it myself, read my own
symptoms, act on them in time, and stay within my
limits. But at present I'm afraid I don't have any idea
of how successful I'm going to be at catching myself in
time, and it's no use pretending I'm confident of
getting it right. This does mean that to begin with I
don't see how I could take on home visiting, and you
may well feel this rules me out.'

'Oh, I don't see why it should.' For the first time

Amrit Patel intervened. 'We've been handling them without you until now quite satisfactorily, so I see no reason why we can't go on doing so. You would be an extra pair of hands in any case, we'd have your help in morning and evening surgery, and I gather the idea is that you'd take over nearly all our work at Vicky's — that's our cottage hospital on the other side of the road. That would all make a big difference, it seems to me.'

'I agree. I'm sure we can go on coping with the home visits,' Gina said at once. 'Nothing to it.'

George was looking smug now, instead of furious.

'In any case,' Ross told them, 'I do think that as I get used to pacing myself I should be able to take on some home visiting. In a month or two, maybe.'

'However,' James pointed out firmly, 'we can't count on that, can we?'

Ross opened his mouth, but James didn't wait for his reply. 'All right, it's likely you'll learn how to deal with the problem. But what if you don't? What if these episodes continue indefinitely? What then?'

'Fair enough. A perfectly valid point. So how about if I were to join you for a trial period — three months, say, or six months, to give you time to look for someone else? That way all of us would have a clearer idea of how useful I can be before we take any final decision.'

'Once we've got you,' George said forcefully, 'I see no prospect of any of us wanting to let you go. In my opinion — ' he glared belligerently across at James. ' — we're extraordinarily lucky to have the chance of getting anyone like Ross to join us, and it seems to me that to talk of a trial period, as if he were on some sort of probation, is outrageous. An insult.' His colour rose again, and his breath came fast.

'Sorry, George, but I think Ross is wise to suggest the trial period. For one thing it should take any pressure off him, and for all our sakes I think we should accept his offer. Let me do a recap. What it seems to be is that if Ross joins us — and I'm sure there's no doubt whatever that we'd all like him to — he'll help us with our workload here in surgery and at clinics, and see our patients in Vicky's most of the time. Incidentally, Ross, what we don't seem to have mentioned so far is that that would involve an evening round, lateish — after evening surgery. How does that strike you?'

'That'd be fine. I'm not unused to working unsocial hours.' He grinned. 'It might even be an advantage. I don't need to go early to bed or anything of that kind. All I need is to be able to pace myself a bit, have a lie-down during the day as well as fit in an exercise work-out, around midday, if possible. So if I took a bit of time off then, and paid it back by doing a late round at the hospital, that would suit me.'

'Good. So what do you all think of this suggestion? First of all, if Ross has no objection, I'd like the two of us to have a quiet chat privately, and go over his medical history in rather more detail. After that, evening surgery, and then I know George is taking Ross home to Rose Bank for a meal. How would it be if you stick to that programme, George, while Amrit and Gina and I have a little discussion among ourselves, and decide how things are going to work out best for all concerned? I do rather feel——' he rode determinedly over the threat of another angry outburst from George '—that we should allow ourselves to spend a wee bit of time on this question. I agree with you, George, entirely, that we'll be lucky to have Ross here with us, but equally I'm sure we owe it to ourselves and to Ross to assess exactly where we all stand and what we are taking on.'

Gina cut in abruptly. 'I agree with Dad, actually. I don't see why there need be any argument about it. We can have him join us, and count ourselves lucky. But if Ross agrees to your proposal, I've no objections, and I'll talk it over with you after surgery if that's what you want — though I'll only repeat what I've just said.'

'What James suggests is very sensible, and the best for each of us, I think,' Amrit said. 'If Ross has no objection, I certainly have not.'

Ross hurriedly said he'd be very glad to talk to James privately, and to carry out the rest of his plan. 'And I'm very much in favour of a three-month trial. It would take the pressure off me, and be to my advantage as much as anyone's. If I found I couldn't cope with the standing, I wouldn't feel I was letting you down, if we'd agreed in advance to this trial period.' At this, even George gave in, and the meeting broke up, Ross accompanying James to his consulting room across the hall.

CHAPTER TWO

WHEN evening surgery was over, George, who appeared to have made up his mind that Ross would be joining the practice, insisted on taking him upstairs to see the flat at the top of the house that went with the job.

'Betty Armstrong has the first-floor flat,' he explained, leading the way to the lift. 'Up we go. It's pretty ancient, this old thing, but reliable. They put it in when the senior partner lived here in this house, on the two upper floors, way back in the twenties.'

Ancient was the word, Ross thought, as they rose with shudders and rumbles past the first floor and on up to the second.

'Once you're here, you're self-contained,' George told him. 'The place is a bit spartan, though, but we leave it fairly bare deliberately, so that occupants can make it over in their own style. You're welcome to use it, but if you'd rather stay on at the Rose and Crown, or in one of the Northborough guest houses, don't hesitate to say.' As he talked he was leading the way round the flat, opening and shutting doors, and Ross glimpsed a small kitchen, more of a pantry than anything else, a much larger bathroom — once a bedroom, he guessed — two more bedrooms with dormer windows, and a pleasant sitting-room overlooking the garden, with French windows on to a balcony with a fire escape.

'It seems most liveable-in, Ross assured him. 'I'd be glad to take it over.'

'Our cleaning lady would go through it once a week for you. Betty Armstrong will arrange it for you and tell you what the charge is. And Betty would see to your food and main meals if you ask her — she's always prepared to run the catering for this flat. What it means in practice is that you get a plateful of whatever she and her daughter are having each evening, and she keeps your fridge and store cupboard stocked up with basics. She makes a weekly charge, of course, but you'd find it very reasonable.'

'Sounds like the lap of luxury.'

'There's no doubt we're lucky to have her. She runs the practice on oiled wheels. Now, we'd better be off. Daphne's expecting us for a meal.' He led the way back to the ancient lift, down and then out to the porch. 'That's Vicky's, over there,' he gestured across the road. 'Our own general practitioner cottage hospital. Right on the spot, as you can see.'

They drove in the big old Bentley out of the centre of Northborough to a wide tree-lined avenue with grass verges and an air of prosperity, turned up a drive and halted before a low two-storeyed Edwardian house, gabled and creeper-hung

'I'll leave the car out,' George said. 'We'll need it again later.'

Daphne Hurst, tiny and elegant in a flowery suit, was welcoming, though her eyes, as green as her daughter's, watched him a trifle warily, almost as though he might suddenly bite, he thought.

'Do come in, Dr Nicholson, I've been so looking forward to meeting you. Or should it be Mr Nicholson? George did say——'

'What it should be is Ross.'

'And I'm Daphne. That's much nicer. Come along in.' She preceded him across a square spacious hall into a sitting-room with wide sofas and chairs covered in yellow brocade, more yellow at the windows, bowls of yellow tulips and daffodils everywhere.

'Sit yourself down and talk to George, while I check up on our meal.'

'Can I do anything?'

'No, no, all under control. Or at least I hope so, I'm just going to make sure. So sit yourself down with George, and relax. Pay no attention to me.'

She wasn't, though, the most relaxing of hostesses.

'Now, Ross, what'll you drink?'

Ross asked for whisky, George had the same, and poured a sherry for his wife, who carried it off to the kitchen with her.

'Cheers!' George raised his glass, and took a deep swallow as though he needed it. 'Now, first things first,' he said. 'Let's be frank with one another. Having met my partners, what do you feel about joining us here?'

'Surely it's much more how you all feel about having me — with my disability.' He had to force the final word through his lips. Ridiculously, he knew, he always hated having to admit to any physical handicap.

'We'd be lucky to have you, as I've said from the outset. But James has chosen to be difficult, as if we're doing you some sort of favour. Nonsense. I've no doubt whatever you can tackle the job, but do you still want it?'

'There does remain the problem of my wonky back, and — '

'Of course there does, but that's why you're here in the first place, isn't it? And I'm sure we'll be able to work out a regime that allows you to help us a great deal but still remain within your present capacities. And James and the other two are bound to come to the same conclusion, it's a dead certainty. So I'm asking you, do you still want to join us?'

'I'd be glad to. I had a good talk with James, you know, before sitting in on surgery with you, and we got on fine. I rather took to him. As long as he and the others feel I can do the job, I'm ready to take it on whenever you like.'

'Good. I'm delighted to hear it. Welcome aboard. How about starting next week. Monday?'

'Sure. By all means. No problem.'

'Fine. We'll wait for James's call to confirm it, of course, but speaking for myself I'll say here and now that I very much look forward to having you working with us.' The telephone on the coffee-table rang, and he picked it up. 'Yes. Good. I knew you would. Yes, quite right, I'm sure we can. I'll tell him.' He put the telephone down. 'That was James, as you no doubt gathered. He says they're all three agreed they'd like you to join us. So that's settled. We'll stick to the three month trial on both sides, though personally I don't see the necessity for it. All right?'

'Very much all right. I look forward to working with you and the other partners.' Except for one of them, of course.

'For myself, I'm delighted. I shall be able to take life more easily, and have more time off. Daphne will be pleased.'

He was right about this. Over their meal, his wife expressed at some length her pleasure that Ross would be joining the practice, and her relief that pressure for George could be reduced. 'I'm particularly anxious that he should give up this rubbish about being on call twenty-four hours a day, seven days a week. I'm relying on you, Ross, to put a stop to it.' Her mouth set in a determined little line as she faced him across

the round table set in the bay window of what they
had told him was their breakfast-room, though they
used it as a dining-room for all but the largest and
most formal dinner parties. She was almost glaring
across it, the green eyes snapping, first at Ross and
then, accusatorily, at her husband. 'I mean it, George,'
she said. 'You've got to stop working all the hours
there are. It has to end, and now's your opportunity,
with Ross here to help.'

'It's never seven days a week,' George protested.
'Five and a half, occasionally six, maybe. But not
seven. You mustn't exaggerate.'

'I'm not. I only wish I were.' She turned to Ross
again. 'He may not be officially on call for seven days,
but I assure you he's on the telephone, even if he's off
duty at home. He's never free from the demands of
the practice. Never. And it's got to stop. Otherwise
it's going to kill him.'

'Oh, come on, Daph. You mustn't dramatise like
this.' George was conciliatory but firm. 'A few extra
telephone calls aren't going to hurt me, and you
mustn't tell yourself they are. All you're doing is
upsetting yourself over a quite minor problem. Long
hours, after all, are the nature of the job, and always
have been. I'm used to it, and——'

'I know you're used to it, but you shouldn't be. It's
not good for you, George, and if you don't call a halt
it easily could kill you. I know I'm right about this,
and it's not drama, unfortunately. It's reality.'

'Now, Daph, that's enough.' Suddenly there was
steel in his voice, a good deal to Ross's surprise. 'Don't
ruin our digestions. Ross understands the situation,
and he'll see my time on call is reduced. So let's leave
it at that.'

Daphne glared across at her husband, but she tightened her lips and, again to Ross's surprise, obediently changed the subject. 'Do you think you'll be able to manage in the top-floor flat?' she enquired anxiously. 'I'm afraid it's dreadfully shabby, and the furniture is mainly our throw-ous.'

'It's fine,' he assured her. 'Streets ahead of the usual temporary accommodation on offer, do believe me.'

'It isn't at all what I'd like to be able to offer you,' she said. 'The thing is, we've rather let it go, you see, because assistants nearly always arrive these days with wife and family and a good deal of furniture of their own, so now, you see, it's embarrassingly basic, and not in the least what you're used to, I'm sure. And I don't see what we can do about it, because all the good bits and pieces we could spare from here went into the flat over the garage that Gina has taken over.' She pleated the edge of the damask tablecloth with nervy fingers, while Ross envisaged the repercussions if Dr Georgina Hurst came home to find her own flat raided and denuded of furniture for his benefit.

He set out to be reassuring, listing the advantages of the attic flat—its proximity to the surgery and to Vicky's, the lift, and, especially, the big bathroom. 'It's vast, and that's going to be immensely useful as far as I'm concerned. I have to do a lot of exercises for my back, and I cart round apparatus for this. I'll be able to put it into the bathroom, and do my exercises there.'

Daphne cheered up slightly. 'In the old days, I believe, that was the nursery floor. That's why it has this big bathroom, made out of a bedroom, but only a tiny pantry kitchen used just for heating up hot drinks, filling hot water bottles and so on. There would have been nannies, and nurserymaids, and meals sent up from the kitchen in the basement.'

'Fine for me, anyway. And George says Betty
Armstrong will feed me, so I'm going to be thoroughly
well looked after. I shall be in clover.' He smiled at
her encouragingly, though he could already see
nothing was going to stop her worrying, and he began
to see exactly why Leo had assured him that if George
Hurst was doing him a favour there wasn't the slightest
doubt that Ross would be doing him one in return.

An obsessional worrier Daphne might be, but she
was also a fabulous cook. While the arguments had
been going on, they had eaten course after delicious
course — smoked haddock mousse with hard-boiled
egg, a notable game casserole, and finally a creamy
and mouthwatering gooseberry and elderflower fool.

Daphne, though, had discovered a new cause for
anxiety. 'You look as if you could do with a bit of
feeding up, Ross,' she informed him maternally.
'You're really dreadfully thin.'

'Betty Armstrong can see to that,' George intervened briskly. 'And now, my dear, I think perhaps we
should——'

'Coffee,' she said at once. 'That's right. You have it
in the study. I'll bring it through shortly.'

'Can't I help with anything?' Ross protested, though
he already knew her well enough to be sure his offer
would be turned down. 'This has been the most
magnificent meal——'

'Oh, I'm so glad you enjoyed it.' She smiled delight-
edly, and for a moment looked years younger.

'I haven't enjoyed a meal so much for ages. But do
let me help you to clear, take——'

'Oh, no.' She was flustered again. 'No, no, there's
not the slightest need, and the kitchen's a shambles
anyway.' She waved her hands about in the nervous
gestures rapidly becoming familiar to him. 'I'll be

perfectly all right on my own—I—I like to take my time, you see, and then I don't get in a muddle. You go along with George,' she added urgently.

Ross followed George into the study—more a consulting room than a personal study, it seemed. A big desk took up the window space, two upright chairs opposite it, while on the far side of the room were two comfortable leather armchairs with a table between them. An examination couch stood against one wall, a glass-fronted cabinet of instruments and drugs against the other, together with a tall book case jammed to overflowing with textbooks and back numbers of the *British Medical Journal.'*

'Daph worries, you know,' George explained unnecessarily. 'About me, I mean.'

Ross was blunt. 'Maybe she has reason. Let's talk about you instead of me for a change. You told me a certain amount about your health when we had dinner with Leo that evening. But just how much angina are you actually getting—say this week, for instance?'

George was evasive. 'Oh, well, you know, it varies. Some days I get away with it, not a twinge.'

'And some you don't.'

'True. But I carry Trinitrate, and it always responds to that.'

'Look, George, obviously, just as Daphne says, you have been doing too much, not getting enough relaxation. I see why she's worried, but what I'd like to know is, are you worried yourself?'

George frowned. 'Hard to say, really. It varies. I am sometimes—if I've had a bad day, for instance. Then I start totting up the arrangements I ought to have made. On one of those occasions I got on to Leo, and the result is here you are with us, and I've definitely reduced my workload. So I may live.' He chuckled, apparently with genuine good humour. 'I used to worry a good deal about Daph, but I don't need to now Gina's back. She'll look after her mother whatever happens—she would have done anyway, of course, but now she's living here, which is a very different matter from being involved up to her eyebrows at Mortimer's.'

So madam came from Mortimer's, did she?

'You've made your dispositions, sure. And very wise. But what I really want——'

The telephone rang. George picked it up. 'Dr Hurst.' His face lit up. 'Yes, darling, of course. Carry on.'

Ross was intrigued. Who was this? The dialogue at George's end was hardly informative, consisting mainly of monosyllables—yes, no, quite—and occasional phrases, such as I agree entirely, yes, indeed, much better, or, once or twice, yes, you could try that. His face, though, continued to give him away. Whoever he was talking to was the light of his life. As the conversation went on Ross realised something else. The person he was talking to was a colleague. He was saying, 'Right, then, see how she goes along now you've got her in. I'll look in on her when I come over—no, no, of course I'm coming over as usual tonight. See you then, darling.' He replaced the telephone and turned back to Ross. 'That was Gina,' he explained happily.

So it was Pinstripe who was the light of his life. His beloved daughter. He should have guessed, Ross told himself. After all, he'd seen from the outset that she was someone's darling daughter, hadn't he? Except, of course, he hadn't for a moment supposed she'd turn out to be his own senior partner's daughter. George's one and only ewe-lamb. He'd have to watch it.

George was telling him about Gina's patient. 'A teenager with cystic fibrosis,' he said. 'Susie Winter.' He sighed. 'Known her all her life — brought her into this world myself, sixteen years ago, and a hard time she's had of it, poor kid. I didn't do her any favours, I sometimes think, delivering her safely. At first I thought we'd never bring her through her childhood, let alone her teens. She's done better than I dared to hope in those early days.'

Cystic fibrosis was a hereditary condition, and babies born with it had problems with breathing and with digestion, so from the beginning they failed to thrive. Not so long ago, many of them died in childhood, their lungs so damaged that they never knew what it was not to be short of breath. Their hearts had a constant struggle to keep the circulation going, until finally the day inevitably came when both heart and lungs lost the battle.

'Luckily,' George went on, 'our knowledge of the condition has grown with Susie, so that the outlook for her now is immensely more hopeful than it was at her birth. Well, we'll pop into Vicky's — Gina's just admitted her there; she's picked up another infection, poor wee lassie. You can see her for yourself. I'm worried about her.'

'I'll be interested to see her. I've been dealing with a fair number of these patients with cystic fibrosis at the Central, as a matter of fact.'

'You have? Oh, excellent. You and Gina can have a good talk about Susie, a mini case-conference.' George beamed.

Ross was saved from replying, as Daphne came in with a tray of coffee, which she put down on the table between George and Ross. 'I'll leave you to pour for yourselves,' she told them, and departed as quickly as she'd come.

George poured coffee, and Ross returned to their earlier conversation — he wanted to know more about George's heart condition before he began working with him daily. He took the coffee George handed him. 'Thank you. Now, George, may we get back to you and your own health? I was asking you, if you remember, whether you are worried about it yourself?'

George grinned lopsidedly. 'Exactly as John Hunter put it over two hundred years ago, "My life is in the hands of any rascal who chooses to annoy and tease me." Absolutely true for me today, and I must say I don't altogether care for it.'

A huge understatement, that had to be. So he was worried. 'Are you — um —— ' Ross hesitated. 'Would you say you can be fairly easily upset — do you get angry easily?'

'I can do. Mostly I don't, otherwise I'd never have survived in general practice, would I? But of course every day brings its problem patients, and I've always been apt to be a bit too quick off the mark. Alternatively, I try hard not to be, and the result is I boil away inside. Neither of which is good for my heart, as I'm well aware. But the trouble is, when I leave here in the morning I can be quite philosophical, ready to handle everyone and everything, no problem. As the day wears on, though, I do tend to get short-tempered and snappy.'

'Don't we all? I do see, though, why Daphne worries about your long hours. And this late round at Vicky's does mean you're routinely working a very long day.'

'Well, I'm handing that over to you, aren't I? And with you here, things can only get better. However, while we're here on our own, one point I would like to make clear. Suppose I do have a coronary—and we have to accept it's quite on the cards I could, one of these days—then I don't want anyone to allow me to be rushed off by ambulance to intensive care at St Mark's in Halchester. It's a very good hospital, don't think it isn't, and I have the greatest respect for its doctors and nurses, but that's not how I want to end my days, strung up to ventilators and drips, dedicated staff struggling to prolong my life for another twenty-four hours if at all possible. I don't want a long-drawn-out terminal illness. I've had a good life, all things considered, and I'm ready to go when my time comes. So if I should have a heart attack here at home, or on my rounds, by all means let me be moved into Vicky's, but that's the limit. Understood? If I come through, then, fine, I'll go over to St Mark's and Kenneth Gray, the cardiologist there, can investigate me and advise me. But I'm not to be hustled over there in a moribund condition, blue light flashing, at the last moment minus one. James understands this, and now I've told you, too. All right?'

'I understand how you feel, of course. But I do have to remind you, strung up in Intensive Care, you might well live to fight another day, and be thankful. As I was. I spent weeks being run by machinery—no one consulted me, they slung me into Intensive Care and battled to keep me alive. If they'd asked me I would have said no. Enough is enough. Finish. But no one did ask me. And if they had, I wouldn't be here now. So are you one hundred per cent sure you really want to turn your back on what technology and medical skill have to offer in the way of life-saving care?'

'You're a young man, Ross. In your thirties, yes?'

'Thirty-four.'

'There's the difference. I'm sixty-four. Vicky's for me, no further. And don't you and James forget it.'

'I won't forget. But with any luck it's not going to come to this. You have been changing your lifestyle, haven't you. Didn't you say you'd cut out smoking?'

'Oh, yes, way back — though I used to be a twenty-a-day man, I'm afraid.'

'And you've been slimming, is that right?'

'I have, though that's not entirely straightforward.'

'After tonight's meal I can well believe you. It was terrific.'

'Yes, well, that's it. Daph has always been a perfectly splendid cook, and she finds it difficult to adjust to the idea that I need to lose weight. She's geared to building people up — as you saw for yourself this evening — and she still inwardly sees herself as a failure unless I eat like a horse. Like several horses. However, I have managed to lose the odd pound, and I keep plugging away.'

'Exercise?'

George shook his head. 'Far too little, I have to admit. A round of golf twice a week, grass-cutting — but with a motor mower — and a bit of gardening in the summer, and there you have it.'

'Have you thought of an exercise bike, or a rowing machine, or maybe a treadmill — whichever suits you best — for use indoors all the year round?'

George laughed shortly. 'Kenneth Gray asked me that, you know. But I thought he was a bit over the top. You think it's a good notion, do you?'

'I must say I find my own exercise bike invaluable. However, no rush. The main thing is for you to ease up and reduce your hours, which you're about to do. And that in itself will give you more time for exercise — say another round of golf? And some walking in the summer evenings, perhaps.'

'Everything's going to change now you're going to be here. Another pair of hands, no late round at Vicky's — no morning round either, unless you specifically need me to look at someone. That's the object of our arrangement. I shall take things easy and be a reformed character, eating much less and exercising far more.'

'I'll keep reminding you of that. I have an uneasy suspicion that I may have quite a struggle to take over as much as I should.' The dark eyes glinted, and Ross raised a quizzical eyebrow. 'These Type A personalities — all the same. Can't let up.'

George twinkled happily, ready to share the joke against himself. 'I am not a Type A personality,' he said with mock gravity. 'I'm an equable family doctor, a bit overweight, true, and with rather too heavy a workload, so I'm getting a touch of angina now and again. But you're going to shift the workload, I'll start shedding the pounds and that'll be it. You'll see.'

Ross shook his head. 'A Type A personality if ever I met one,' he retorted jokingly. But he knew it was only too true. George was conscientious, striving, a bit of a perfectionist. What was more, he shared his life with the tense and over-anxious Daphne, who wanted all her meals eaten and appreciated. A recipe for a coronary, Ross feared.

CHAPTER THREE

IT WAS well after ten when George drove Ross back into the town centre, and drew up outside Vicky's, which turned out to be a red-brick Victorian mansion with spacious grounds, vivid where the street light caught them with spring bulbs swaying in the windy night.

'We're rather proud of Vicky's,' George said 'We had one hell of a fight to keep it—the NHS scheduled it for closure ten years ago—but what seemed like the entire population of Northborough got involved in our campaign to retain it, and as a result the League of Friends is never short of volunteers. A retired bank manager looks after our finances, and an ex-headmaster runs the garden—he's moved into a flat, but as he's a keen gardener he's in his element running teams who mow, sweep, spray the roses and weed. As far as I can make out, he seldom does a hand's turn himself. His forte is pinning up lists on the noticeboard, and strolling about the place pointing here and there.'

'A great gift, if you have it,' Ross commented drily.

They moved into a broad hall with a receptionist's counter, unmanned, and along a corridor. 'This is it,' George said. 'The hub of this particular universe. Sister's office. Katrine Fremantle is our sister-in-charge, and I'll introduce you to her on Monday. We have two night sisters who job-share and divide the week between them. One's a widow in her sixties, Abby Maitland, and the other a single parent in her twenties—they seem to get along fine, and give us a splendid service. One of them will be around some-where. This is a fairly free and easy place, more a sort of convalescent home than a hospital really, where the locals can be admitted when they need a bit more nursing care than we can arrange at home for them. We take patients from the day surgery unit at St Mark's when necessary, and a good many Northborough patients come back here after a week or two in the acute surgical wards to complete their recuperation.'

'Sounds an immensely useful set-up,' Ross said.

'It is.' It was George's turn to assess Ross, and he realised his new recruit was nearing total exhaustion. The sooner he was in his bed in the Rose and Crown the better, he decided, revising his earlier plans hastily. 'It's far later than I thought,' he remarked. 'We must have been talking much longer than I realised, so I'll just give you a quick overview of how the system here works from this office, and then on Monday we'll do a proper round together, with Sister. This is the bed-state.' He gestured towards the big blackboard on the wall. 'The different coloured chalks tell you which doctors are responsible for which beds — our practice is blue — here, you see, in blue, is our cystic fibrosis girl, Susie. I see she's on her own in the twin-bedded ground-floor ward. Sensible, that. She can go on having physio through the night, and do a good cough each time without disturbing anyone. Next door you'll find our little intensive care ward, and next to that our pride and joy, the resuscitation room, recently funded by the League of Friends. We think it's going to prove life-saving. It's half an hour, you see, minimum, by ambulance to St Mark's, more in the rush hour, and double that for the round trip. You can easily lose a patient who could have been saved with immediate admission.'

'That was our argument for going out to road accidents with a surgical team,' Ross responded.

'Well, we can get patients in here much faster than we can get them to St Mark's, and we're quite proud of the equipment we've managed to acquire. The only thing is, we don't have piped oxygen. But we're always well stocked with cylinders, and——' He broke off, as voices sounded in the corridor, heralding the entrance of a grey-haired nursing sister, accompanied by Gina.

'Hello, Dad,' she said cheerfully. 'I've done the late round, so you can be off home again *stat*. Nothing to report, is there, Abby?'

'No, everyone's quite comfortable, and most of them sound asleep.'

'Susie seems a bit better after her physio, and Abby's going to give her chest a good pummelling every two hours. So I suggest you go straight back home to bed, and w. can have our talk about her on Monday, when we can see how's she's responded.' Both men looked exhausted, Gina thought, and over-due for a good night's rest. Momentarily, she even began to have second thoughts over having supported Ross's inclusion in the practice so enthusiastically— how much of a support was he going to be for her overworked father?

George was never to be hurried. He stayed to intro-duce Ross formally to Abby, telling her that he would be joining the practice as from Monday morning. 'You can expect to see a lot more of him, I'm glad to say.' He turned to his daughter. 'Thank you for doing the round, my dear. Ross and I will call it a day. Come on, Ross, I'll drop you off at the Rose and Crown.'

'No, no. I can make my own way,' Ross assured him

at once. 'I can totter that far without collapse, I should hope.'

'You go straight home, Dad, and I'll drive Ross,' Gina put in firmly.

'Look, I mean it. No way do I need a lift from anyone. It's barely a hundred yards. It's very good of you both, but no. Not necessary.'

'My dear lad, of course we shouldn't dream of expecting you to walk there at the end of a hard day. What nonsense.' George overruled him promptly. 'Off you go with Gina. She can bring you up to date on Susie—we've been talking about her already, darling, so you can carry on where I left off, and then all three of us can have a case-conference over her on Monday, how's that?' He kissed his daughter, patted Ross encouragingly on his broad shoulder, said goodnight to Abby, picked up his bag, and set off down the hall. The doors swung behind him.

'There's honestly not the slightest need——' Ross began.

'Of course I'll drive you. No problem. It must have been a very long day for you, anyway,' Gina added kindly, not for an instant suspecting that no remark could have been more guaranteed to irritate Ross.

He set his teeth. No mistaking it, this impossible woman had now switched roles, and she was not only going to patronise him intolerably but apparently intending to wrap him in cotton wool on the slightest provocation. This he would stop.

Not tonight, though, he decided reluctantly. They could hardly stand about squabbling and snapping at each other in front of the night sister, when he'd only just been introduced to her as the newest acquisition to the Hurst practice. So he smiled frostily and lied through his teeth, though it cost him. 'Most kind of you. If you're sure it's not an imposition.'

'No trouble at all, and the car's right outside. No distance,' she assured him, smiling widely and encouragingly at him, her amazing green eyes looking straight into his.

He was shaken. As her teaching hospital could have informed him, Gina Hurst's smile had been known to stop strong men — including raging consultants on the warpath — in their tracks. It stopped Ross, too, and left him, extraordinarily, short of breath. Bemused, he said a polite goodnight to Abby, and followed Gina along the hall and out to the Jaguar.

In no time at all they drew up outside the Rose and Crown. 'Would you care to come in for a drink?' Ross felt compelled to offer, more formally than with any expectation that she'd accept. 'Or would you,' he added hopefully, 'prefer to — I do realise it's a bit late, and —'

'No, I'd love a drink. It's not that late, anyway — it was just that I wanted to get Dad off home,' she said quickly. This was her chance, and she was grabbing it. She'd behaved abominably in the lane that morning, and she owed Ross an apology. Much better to get it out of the way tonight, so that they could start with a clean slate on Monday. After surgery that evening, when they'd all three discussed Ross, she'd explained what had happened and James had agreed that she should probably apologise as soon as possible.

'I was in the wrong, you know,' she'd admitted to James and Amrit. 'What he said was true. I was going too fast, and I only just managed to stop without doing any damage to either car. I do usually have that lane to myself, but that's no excuse. What I can't forgive myself for, though, is that I never spotted anything

wrong with his back. Here I am, supposed to be a
doctor, but I didn't notice a thing wrong with his gait
or his movements. Now, though, looking back, I can
remember clearly that before he walked round the car
he pushed himself up off it with both hands, and his
walk is a bit deliberate, with his spine held unusually
upright and immobile, isn't it? But I was in too much
of a temper to notice what was straight in front of my
eyes. When I think what he must have been through —
years and years of treatment before he could get back
to work, and then he's a surgeon, isn't he, and he's
never going to be fit enough to work long hours in an
operating theatre. It's tragic. It must have been the
end of the world to him. And all I could do was stand
over him and bawl him out. I'm so ashamed of myself.'

'I dare say, but just tell him you're sorry and leave
it at that, is my advice,' James had told her. 'No need
to make a production out of it — that'll only embarrass
him.'

They walked into the Rose and Crown.

'The bar? Or the lounge?' Ross asked her. 'You
know this place better than I do.'

'The lounge would be more peaceful. I don't know
about you, but I could do with a bit of peace and
tranquillity. Today seems to have been going on for
ever.' Oh dear, hardly tactful. 'It's just that it started
rather early, with a call before breakfast,' she added
hastily.

'Some days can be like that,' he agreed, leading the
way across the room to some free chairs on the far
side. They sat down. 'What would you like to restore
you?' he enquired. 'A large brandy?'

'Help!' Her amazing smile jolted him again. 'I'm not
that far gone. And I do have to drive home, too. I
think I'd better just have an orange juice.' A pity,

though, she reflected. A large brandy would have helped her no end to make her apology, which she was beginning to dread.

He was grinning at her. 'Undoubtedly healthy,' he said. 'But it's not exactly going to set you up, is it? They seem to be serving coffee still—would you like that instead?'

'Just the job. I'd love it.'

He ordered coffee for them both, it came quickly, and he poured it. 'Sugar? Milk?'

'Neither, thank you. Black.'

He passed her the cup and saucer.

'Thank you so much. Just what I need.' She relaxed, stretched her legs out and crossed them at the ankles, and reached for her coffee.

She had changed out of the formal pinstripe, and looked altogether more human, he thought, in her present outfit of trousers, shirt and a padded waistcoat, with a heavy gold chain that swung as she moved. Watching her, for the first time Ross found her friendly and approachable. He must forget about their first meeting, put it behind him and make a new beginning. They were going to be colleagues, working together every day, and this was the moment to start building bridges.

Only he couldn't do it. He clenched his jaw as the recollection of sitting in young Andy's old heap and being pushed along the lane by this smug creature surfaced again and took possession of him. He tried hard to reject the memory. Snap out of it, he told himself fiercely. Put it behind you, once and for all. Catching his steely features and the granite set of his jaw, Gina copped out. She opened her mouth to speak, but what came out was not the apology she'd been planning. An olive branch, perhaps, but not an apology. A failure of nerve at the last moment.

'Dad said something about having spoken to you about Susie, our cystic fibrosis patient?' She knew she was stalling for time, but anything else seemed beyond her.

'He said he'd take me into see her tonight, but I'm afraid, what with one thing and another, we got late. I look forward to seeing her on Monday, though.'

'Officially Dad's handed her over to me, you know—she's on my list. But he's still very much involved with her.' Gina was feeling her way, her mind half on Susie and her father.

'He told me he brought her into the world sixteen years ago, so I suppose it's natural he should want to keep in touch.'

'Yes, but—well, first of all, just how familiar are you with this condition?'

Ross wanted to hit her. Who did she think she was, shooting questions at him as if they were on a teaching round? Easy. A lady from Mortimer's, a hospital renowned for its inflated opinion of itself. At Mortimer's anyone from anywhere else existed in outer darkness, and was more than likely to be stone-age primitive.

'At the Central we are not wholly unfamiliar with the condition.' He was freezing.

Gina was furious with herself. The last thing she'd intended was to antagonise him. Hurriedly she back-tracked. 'I just thought,' she offered weakly, 'that maybe you might not have come across it since you were a student. After all, accident surgeons——'

'Are not wood from the neck up.' From freezing he'd moved to scorching. 'In fact, as it happens,' he prepared to demolish her, 'while I've been at the

Central over the last year or so I've been keeping the records for Tom Rennison's heart-lung transplant programme. At one time I was his registrar, so I actually saw much more of the clinical side of the programme than an average administrator.' That should put this uppity woman in her place. You couldn't get much more high-powered than the Central's heart-lung transplant programme.

However, to his astonishment, far from being put down, Gina showed only delight. 'Then you will have seen something of a patient of ours from Mortimer's,' she told him, locking in at once and forgetting everything but the patient under discussion. 'Rennison operated on her very successfully. She was older than Susie, in her early twenties, and fearfully breathless and disabled.'

'Yes, I remember. Her lung capacity was so reduced that even at her best she couldn't manage a ten-yard walk. The problem with her was whether she'd be able to stand up to surgery, but we went ahead, and she did well.'

'Well, you'll find Susie can do a good deal more than that, and she's fitter generally. But she is deteriorating, and I feel the time has come for her to be referred to a London teaching hospital. The problem, is, Dad is dead against it. He doesn't want her to get caught up in what he calls space-age medicine, which he loathes on principle. He wants her to stay here and be looked after cosily in her own home or at Vicky's when necessary for as long as possible, as long as we can keep her going, so to speak, and after that accept that nature may have to take its course. He means well; by his lights he's only being protective.'

It all fitted, Ross thought. George was not advocating anything for this young patient that he wouldn't prescribe for himself.

'One of the things Dad is against,' Gina was saying, 'is that if Susie did have a transplant, she'd have to be on drugs for the rest of her life. As she's on non-stop drugs now, I can't see that makes so much difference. Oh, I'm so glad you've been in on this transplant programme, it's going to be tremendously useful if you can talk to him about it. At the Central, too.' Her green eyes were suddenly alight with laughter. 'As far as Dad's concerned, the Central has it over Mortimer's any day of the week.'

Ross managed not to say that he felt exactly the same.

'One of the problems has been that he thinks I'm applying attitudes learned on the professorial medical unit at Mortimer's to an innocent and unsuspecting chick he's cared for satisfactorily all her life at home in the bosom of her ever-loving family.'

She'd been on the professorial unit at Mortimer's, had she? So she was genuinely high-powered, and must have been on her way to the top. What had brought her back here to Northborough and general practice?

Gina was still talking about Susie. 'To him, you see, she's the child he's looked after since her birth. Practically a baby in the nursery. But in fact she's sixteen, she's got a boyfriend, and last autumn she wanted to get married to Jason and find a job in a supermarket, and to hell with the lot of us.' The green eyes sparked again.'

Ross was beginning to enjoy himself. 'Go on,' he urged her. 'Tell all.'

'Well, there was a massive family row about it, and Dad and I both got drawn in, he by the parents, and me by Susie and Jason. If you ask me, she's fearfully lucky to have Jason. He's super. Really super.'

Her face was alight now, she looked warm and involved, a caring family doctor, quite unlike the soulless executive he'd encountered that morning. She couldn't actually be hungry for power, either, whatever he'd thought originally, or she'd never have left Mortimer's. Perhaps, Ross hoped, it was going to be all right after all. He'd be able to put their first meeting behind him genuinely and completely, forget it had ever happened.

Gina was talking about Jason. 'He's very protective with her, but he's fun, too, and they seem to me to have a really great relationship. They're one of those couples that make you glad to be in medicine, so that you're able to help them, and you forget about the long hours and the failures and the everlasting grind and the non-stop shortages. Jason and Susie are what it's all in aid of.' She flushed. 'Listen to me being thoroughy soppy—they'd laugh their heads off at Mortimer's.'

'I don't think it's in the least soppy.' Ross was forceful. 'I know exactly what you mean, and I agree with every word. But go on about Susie and your father.

'The thing is, Susie and Jason are both well aware that her life may be short. They've faced it together. And they're right, aren't they? No blinking it. So they want to be together as adults, not potter about at school for another two years, taking their A levels and living at home with their parents. I understand exactly how they feel, and why, but of course Dad and both lots of parents look on them as a pair of crazy adolescents. But they aren't. They're exceptionally mature. They've had to be, poor kids, and they've both taken on board all the implications of Susie's condition and its outlook. The love they share is real, not some adolescent infatuation—or that's my opinion, but Dad doesn't accept it. No way.'

'It sounds as if they're lucky to have you,' Ross told her, his dark eyes meeting Gina's without any barrier for the first time. 'They could easily have been confronted simply by an embattled older generation who knew best, and no argument about it.'

She nodded immediately. 'You've put your finger on it. There is a generation gap. I'm trying to bridge it—so far without much success.'

'So what is Susie doing? Is she still at school? Has the older generation won on that point?'

'A compromise was reached.' Gina pulled a slightly rueful face.'

Ross was astonished to find her enchanting.

'Jason has left school,' she went on. 'He's in Halchester, as a management trainee in the supermarket where he's been filling shelves since he was fourteen. So he's earning. His parents are deeply disappointed, but resigned. Susie's in Halchester too, when she's fit enough, at a secretarial college, doing a nine-month course, after which she'll look for a job. We managed to talk her out of getting a job straight away in the supermarket with Jason, because she's sensible enough to see, when it's put to her, that a supermarket and meeting the public all day long is not the best place for anyone with cystic fibrosis. She'd pick up infection after infection, and have to be off work more than half the time—and it would do her condition no good whatever. Once she's a trained secretary, though, she'll be able to find a post where she doesn't have to meet the public, and ought to have some chance of regular attendance. Perhaps. I'm not really terribly hopeful about that working out, but it's a step in the right direction.'

'I'll say. And what about the two of them leaving home and getting married?'

Gina grinned a little wickedly. 'A compromise was reached on that one, too, though at times I began to despair that any agreement could ever be achieved.' She ran long-fingered hands through her dark hair. 'I often wanted to knock all their silly heads together. However, somehow it all got sorted out. Susie and Jason have had an engagement party, she's wearing a ring, and both families are reluctantly agreed that when she finishes her secretarial course they can get married. She'll be seventeen then, and Jason eighteen. Susie's father is busy converting the attic floor into a flat for the young couple. So their world is filled with hope.' She shook her head sadly. 'Just so long as we can keep Susie alive.' She spread the long-fingered hands.

Ross was thrown to find he had an urgent need to take them both into his own, and tell her everything was going to be all right. How daft could you get? All he actually did was to remark, mildly, that it seemed to him she had done Susie proud.

'Yes, but where will it lead? Nowhere? I don't know. I truly don't know what would be for the best. Dad could easily be right. Maybe we shouldn't snatch her away and slam her into the rigorous investigations of a transplant programme, with all the agony, and pain, and uncertainty involved — months and months of it, with no let up.'

'Is there a chance that Susie and Jason might welcome the challenge?'

'Oh, yes, you're right there, and I think that in theory they both do already. But that's nothing like actually living the experience, is it? That's where I do have to admit that the older generation may be wiser and more realistic. However nice and supportive the staff may be to you, the fact remains that you're basically a guinea-pig, a laboratory animal—Dad's expression, not mine. But there's truth in it.'

'I don't think it's for you, or for any of us, to play God and decide that Susie should not be offered that opportunity. I know it's hard to propel a teenager into what might turn out to be a failure, but at least the way ahead is open. To decide that it's closed for this patient is, it seems to me, overprotective, which is what you said your father was being.'

'That is what I think,' she agreed. 'Except when I waver.' The brilliant green eyes shot a look of complicity at him.

'At least there is a door Susie can walk through. In cystic fibrosis there's an enormous amount on the go.'

'That's right, there is.' Her mobile face was alive with interest, and Ross watched her expression changing by the second. How could he ever have imagined this brilliant and caring physician to be nothing more than a driving careerist? 'I went to this fascinating one-day conference recently,' she told him. 'At the Institute of Child Health, on cystic fibrosis, and——'

'Oh, were you there? So was I. Terrific, wasn't it?' he asked.

She looked astounded. 'You mean you were there? I never saw you.'

She hadn't said it disbelievingly, Ross knew. More regretfully, and he found he too regretted their non-meeting that day six months ago.

'Isn't all that new genetic material riveting? And so hopeful. With any luck, the next generation won't produce very many like Susie. I've always felt it such a rotten fate to be born with a faulty gene, which means you have no choice whatever, you're stuck with an existence ruled by a disability no one can cure.'

'In the meantime we have just to do our best to palliate the worst effects,' Ross said sadly.

'So many of these kids are fantastic, aren't they? They try so hard to lead normal lives; they never give up. What about those amazing infants practically treating themselves? Cold-bloodedly and effectively looking after themselves, putting in tubes for night-time drips——'

'And pummelling themselves in the chest for postural drainage, instead of relying on others to do it. That's what I'm beginning to wonder about. If you've got Susie in Vicky's for physio, how about training her to do that. I bet she wasn't taught it as a child; it wasn't thought of ten years ago, I don't suppose, but no reason why she couldn't pick up on it now.'

'Oh, yes!' The green eyes blazed. 'You're on, my friend,' she told him, momentarily supposing herself back in the residents' sitting-room in Mortimer's, rather than the lounge of the Rose and Crown in Northborough. 'That girl will do anything you tell her to, you know, she's a real trier,' she said. 'We can hardly start her off tonight, poor poppet, but tomorrow Diana and I can have a go. That's a perfectly splendid idea.' Enthusiastically, she beamed at him, and downed the last of her coffee.

'More coffee?' he asked. It was all he could think of to give her, though he longed to be able to offer her the world on a plate. Why this should be so was beyond him. Perhaps he'd fallen asleep and was dreaming. That had to be it. The day did seem to have been going on for ever, but now he had to be sound asleep and dreaming

'Thank you,' she said, passing her cup across.

Ross filled it and passed it back.

Gina was rummaging in her bag, and out of it, held in her slim fingers, came a battered carton of cigarettes. Looking round the lounge, slightly distracted — she was thinking about Susie, not about what she was doing at all — she missed Ross's shocked incredulity, took out a cigarette and put it to her lips, and then removed it to say, clearly as a formality, 'You don't mind, do you? Oh, and you wouldn't happen to have a light, would you?'

Ross shook his head. He couldn't, or didn't want, to believe his eyes.

'No, well, it doesn't matter, Michael will——' It was Michael, the lounge waiter who had brought their coffee, for whom her eyes were searching, and she caught his attention and gestured. He came across at once. 'Have you got a light, Michael? Ah, thank you so much.' She inhaled deeply, and sank back with a sigh of relief.

'I'm surprised, I must say,' Ross remarked distantly to the far wall, 'to find you smoke. Here we are discussing heart-lung transplants and breathing problems generally, yet you——' He broke off, shaking his head with deliberate incomprehension. He was feeling let down, betrayed almost. How could she? Oh, how *could* she?

'Only off duty, I assure you.' Gina was curt. No way was she going to start making excuses for herself, explain how hard she'd been trying for months to cut it out — that this was why, for instance, she no longer carried a lighter. The green eyes belligerent, she attempted to stare him out. But he looked back at her, she thought, rather as if she were a drug addict in some down-at-heel clinic in an inner-city slum.

'I see,' he said remotely, the granite back in his jaw, the dark eyes quelling.

Her chin lifted. She took another drag, inhaled again. If he was going to challenge her, let him see she was no push-over.

'You inhale, too,' he commented distastefully, and shrugged. 'Pointless, obviously, to draw your attention to facts you know as well as I do.'

He was regarding her as if she was the lowest form of life and he could hardly believe they inhabited the same planet, she decided. She sipped her coffee, which was too hot, and then provocatively took her cigarette back to her mouth and inhaled again.

Ross's control snapped. 'Suicidal?' He didn't give her any opportunity to reply. 'I suppose that would be the explanation for your crazy driving. I assumed at the time that you were bent on annihilating other road users, but perhaps it's yourself you're trying to destroy.' He stopped. Who was being destructive now? he asked himself, as far too late he recognised he was engaged in paying her back for having so ignominiously pushed him along the lane.

The last straw. Absolutely, definitely the last straw. Gina could have cried. Instead, she leant forward, ground out her half-smoked cigarette, picked up her cup and swallowed its contents, scalding her mouth uncomfortably in the process. 'Not to worry,' she informed him coolly. 'No need to disturb yourself on my behalf, I assure you. I am not in the least suicidal. Thank you for the coffee. I'll see you on Monday morning, of course, and meanwhile I'll bear in mind your suggestions about Susie and her treatment. Goodnight.' She departed, head high, shoulders back, across the lounge, smiling brilliantly and unseeingly at Michael as she left.

CHAPTER FOUR

AFTERWARDS, Gina blamed herself. If she'd done as she'd originally planned, and apologised to Ross for her behaviour in the lane earlier, the row might never have blown up. Their meeting would have gone differently — and she might not have ended it by reaching for her cigarettes. What's more, when he'd criticised her smoking, she could at least have been honest. She could have told him how hard she was trying to give it up.

There had always been a side to her smoking that she couldn't easily admit, even to herself. All her life, until now, Gina's father had been a smoker, and though he had always discouraged her from taking up the habit she continued to admire him — and this included his smoking. For years he'd been her role model.

Gina loved her mother, but in an entirely different way. They shared a deep, but well-buried, sense of union that went back to childhood, though nowadays what Gina felt for Daphne consciously was no more than a mildly exasperated affection. With George, it had always been much more. In childhood, she adored him, and she had watched his hands admiringly as he lit up, replaced his lighter, drew on his cigarette. She had continued to watch as he tapped the ash off into the heavy glass ashtray on the coffee table, and she had yearned to be old enough to use her own hands in the same fascinating way. It was grown-up, and admirable. When she smoked now, while the conscious part of her mind saw it as an unpleasant, unhealthy habit that she was going to drop as soon as she could, deep within her still lurked the girl who was, like her father, successfully demonstrating sophisticated adult behaviour. During the last hectic months at Mortimer's she had smoked much more than she thought permissible, and when she was settled in at Northborough she told herself she was going to stop—especially as by then George himself had given up, and she knew she was making it more difficult for him if she lit up in his presence. But when she was vulnerable or exhausted smoking continued to bring comfort and reassurance—George's own comfort, his reassurance, in fact, though she hadn't grasped the connection.

After she reached home on Friday night she would have given almost anything to call back what she already saw as her senseless behaviour. Just when she and Ross had been beginning to get on so well, too, talking about Susie and her treatment. She needed Ross's support there.

Monday would be the beginning of a new week, and she would see to it that she got on with Ross. He was going to change her father's way of life just by being there in the practice, even if his spinal injury prevented him from working long hours. That he might also be going to change her own life had not yet dawned on her.

She would meet him over Susie at Vicky's, that was already arranged. If it was at all possible she had to get him on one side and apologise first. And not only for her driving, either. She owed him an apology now for her childish display of temper that evening, too. What must he be thinking of her? That she was quite impossible, for a guess. From now on she had to handle him with kid gloves, and show him how calm and unruffled she could be, no matter what the provocation. And on no account must she reach for a cigarette at any point.

As Ross came down in the creaking old lift from the attic flat, where he'd spent his first night, he was reminding himself that if Gina Hurst chose to smoke herself into the grave it was nothing whatever to do with him. If she chose to drive that Jag of hers like a maniac, it was none of his business.

He didn't see her in the course of a busy morning surgery when, allocated a small room used at other times as an examination cubicle—it had once been a china pantry—he saw a miscellaneous selection of patients who'd rung in or called too late for an appointment with their usual doctor. They were on the whole a typical group for the time of year—people of all ages with heavy colds or incipient flu that had been building up over the weekend, elderly bronchitics made worse by the damp cold, elderly arthritics in the same situation. It was a miserable spring day, with a surgery full of miserable people

Afterwards Betty told him George was expecting him in his room for morning coffee. James Black was already there, and the three of them talked about the patients Ross had seen. James left to do his visits, while George told Ross they could both go over to Vicky's next. 'I'll do the handing-over round with you and Katie—that's Katrine Fremantle, the sister-in-charge. And then after that we're to meet Gina and the physio over young Susie Winter.'

As they walked across the road to the hospital, George briefed Ross. 'Katrine came to us from St Mark's in Halchester, where she was a ward sister. We're lucky to have her—she's immensely capable. Her problem is that her mother has multiple sclerosis, and is getting increasingly dependent on her. Running an acute ward and coping with that was getting unmanageable, I heard on the grapevine. I stepped in and we succeeded in enticing her to join us here. The quieter post suits her, and we can admit her mother to Vicky's if she's going through a bad patch.'

'Brilliant.' Ross was sincere in his admiration, but he couldn't help wondering what price George paid for keeping his finger on the pulse like this.

They went down the hall at Vicky's, and into the office.

Katrine was a slight blonde, poised and immaculate in dark blue, her hair tucked into a chignon under a starched cap with frilled edges.

George introduced Ross, and explained that from now on he would be taking over most of the care of the practice's patients in Vicky's. 'I want to do a handing-over round now, Katie, if you have a minute.'

It was a good deal more than a minute, though only about eight of the roughly thirty patients in the wards came from the practice. George, though, handed them over at considerable length, chatting them up in a manner that obviously went down well with them, but that Ross could see only too clearly must mean that his hospital rounds ate up a huge amount of his working day. Unmistakably, George was the old type of family doctor who knew not only all about his patients, but the ramifications of their home life, their neighbours and most of their relatives. Now, of course, he was paying the price for this involvement in exhaustion, worry and angina.

After the handing over, they went back to the office and George wrote up the patients they'd seen in the day book, discussing them all, their treatment, their drug dosages, in detail with Ross and Katrine. 'Now they're all yours, Ross,' he said. 'But don't hesitate to consult me at any time if you want to.'

'I won't,' Ross agreed, while vowing inwardly that this would be as infrequently as he could make it.

A doctor from another practice came quickly in, paused momentarily to be introduced to Ross, then went off with Katrine to visit his own patients. No sooner had they disappeared than Gina came in. She was wearing a camel skirt with a matching polo neck, and the padded waistcoat she'd worn on Friday evening, together with her gold chain. She looked capable and businesslike, reminiscent of any young woman doctor in her working gear — though he was already certain that whatever else Gina might be, she'd never, as far as he was concerned, be any young woman doctor. She might be enchanting, or infuriating, or just plain awful. Gina Hurst was entirely unpredictable, but you could count on it, she'd make an impact.

She took off the padded waistcoat at once — like most hospitals, Vicky's was far too hot for all but its most endangered patients — and threw it at one of a row of hooks along the far wall.

'Here you are, darling,' George said. 'Now for Susie. I'll be interested to hear what you think about her, Ross. Gina and I don't exactly see eye to eye, I'm afraid. Another opinion is just what we need.

Gina made no comment on this, saying only that she had to give them the physiotherapist's apologies. 'She isn't able to be with us, after all — she has this eighty-year-old she sees at midday today who gets terribly fussed if her weekly appointment is altered. Apparently physio is followed by Meals on Wheels, and the whole day goes to glory if Diana isn't in and out by twelve-thirty. Anyway, she talked to me earlier about Susie and how she's been over the weekend. She's shown her how to pummel her own chest, and suggested she tries to do it two-hourly at home, whether her mother's around to help or not, and also whenever she wakes in the night. At present Susie has a bit of a way to go, she said — she's not really thumping herself nearly hard enough.'

George snorted irritably. 'Typical physio's comment. None of us ever do anything ferociously enough for them. Main thing is Susie's made a beginning. An excellent plan of yours, Ross.'

So Gina had passed on his suggestion, in spite of her temper at the time. A point in her favour, Ross decided, as the three of them went into the small double ward next to the resuscitation room.

Susie's mother was with her. She jumped up immediately. 'It's all right, Doctor, I was just going anyway,' she said. 'I won't get in your way. Susie's a good deal better, thank goodness — you were quite right, Doctor, to bring her in here, I see that now. Bye for now, love. Back this afternoon.'

Though no one could have called her a raving beauty, Ross thought Susie Winter was loaded with off-beat charm. From behind enormous glasses, slipping down a snub nose, big brown eyes watched the three of them, and though her complexion was pasty, it was clear, her lips full and still childishly vulnerable. She had a defenceless quality that instantly alerted the male protective instinct, and he saw at once why George had qualms about handing her over to strangers.

The three of them examined her in turn, listening to her chest, back and front, peering down her throat, feeling her glands and palpating her abdomen. Ross, since this was his first examination, was even more thorough, wanting to experience for himself what so far he'd merely been told. He spent a particularly long time on her chest, listening through his stethoscope while she sat forward, while she obediently breathed in, breathed out, coughed, and coughed again.

George and Gina, who knew exactly what hideous sounds he was getting from poor Susie's disabled and congested lungs, watched him, nodding to one another at intervals as his detailed examination picked up what they both knew he'd find if he looked in the right place — which he unerringly did.

Susie was a most co-operative patient, knowing from long practice how to respond to the clinician's every request, and Ross found himself experiencing the reward that could so often come under these conditions, the steady building of acceptance and trust, a genuine rapport betwen doctor and patient. This was what he'd missed out on since his spinal injury, but here, on his first morning in general practice, he found it again.

Eventually they left Susie to her lunch — for which in fact they'd made her late — and adjourned again to the office. Here they compared her recent chest X-rays with those taken earlier, looked at her pulmonary function tests — improved since admission, though that wasn't saying a lot, as Gina pointed out — and checked the laboratory reports.

'Blood counts aren't bad,' George said. 'Haemoglobin normal. A bit of iron deficiency, only to be expected, and — '

'She's on fairly high dosages of pancreatic supplement, I suppose?' Ross asked. Although the obvious symptoms of cystic fibrosis were shown in the lungs, as with Susie, the cause lay in the pancreas, which failed to work properly, so that its inadequate output had to be boosted with pancreatic enzyme and vitamins.

'That's right,' George agreed. 'Her liver function isn't impaired, luckily.'

'But if we leave her too long, it jolly well will be,' Gina pointed out.

She was right, too, Ross knew.

George sighed. 'What you mean is that we should get on with referring her to London before she can deteriorate further.'

Gina nodded determinedly. 'Yes, Dad, that is what I mean.' She didn't enjoy opposing George, but she had to battle for Susie. For Susie's life, as she saw it.

'You've brought her through successfully this far,' Ross commented, feeling that even if his judgement was impaired, George needed a bit of support. 'That's an achievement in itself.'

'Things are getting steadily better for patients like Susie with every year that passes,' Gina said. 'Don't you agree, Ross?' Unxpectedly the green blaze switched direction, and she looked straight across into Ross's own dark eyes.

Good grief, she was actually asking him to back her up—and luckily for him he could do so wholeheartedly. 'I certainly do,' he assured her. 'No reason as far as I can see, with today's advances, why Susie shouldn't live on into her twenties and thirties.'

'That's right.' Gina gave Ross her sudden wide and transfiguring smile. 'But it does mean, Dad, that we have to face up to facts. I do honestly think we absolutely must refer her on to a teaching hospital. No more shilly-shallying and putting it off until she's a bit older. A bit older and a bit worse.' She was vehement, and the vivid green flared brilliantly across the little office.

His first day in his new post, Ross thought ruefully, and here was this incredible girl demanding that he help her to overrule the senior partner. Who said general practice would be boring?

'I wish I knew what to do for the best,' George said. He looked helplessly — not to mention hopefully — towards Ross, clearly expecting his support.

Ross saw this, and knew he couldn't give it. 'What exactly is it you have against referral?' he enquired, though he was aware this was no more than a delaying tactic.

'She's so damned young,' George said explosively. 'Once she gets into the hands of a teaching hospital, whether Mortimer's or the Central, we all know that the next step will be starting to consider whether or not she's suitable for a heart-lung transplant. She'll have to go through all those exhausting and stressing investigations that precede that kind of decision. Maybe they decide no, she's not suitable, and all the discomfort and worry will have been for nothing, she's no better off, could have stayed here and been cared for at home. To put her in line for a transplant is such a major step, makes so many, and such far-reaching demands on both patient and family.

'I agree with all that, of course,' Ross began. 'But——'

George was unstoppable. 'Surgeons can be hopelessly over-enthusiastic, too. They manage to remember only their successful cases, where the patient's life has, as they rightly tell us, been transformed. They forget the others, who go through hell and high water, and don't come out at the other end. Surgeons are quick to forget the pain and misery involved in their failures. Or that's how I see it, but Gina looks at it differently.'

'I do think we have to refer her on. She's getting beyond our management here, and beyond St Mark's too.'

'The paediatricians at St Mark's have looked after her from birth,' George told Ross. 'Now she's reached sixteen, though, she mainly sees the chest consultant. I'm afraid I'm a bit apt to feel it's the children's department — and myself, of course — we who've known her from the outset, who fully understand her condition, her strengths and her weaknesses, rather than the chest people who've only recently come into the picture. Yes, yes, I'm well aware — ' he overrode an attempt by Gina to interrupt him ' — this may easily be a bit of a hang-up on my part. I know Gina's talked to the chest man at St Mark's, and he goes along with the idea of referring her to London.' He shrugged. 'So there you are. That's my opinion, for what it's worth.'

Ross heard him out with a schooled, remote expression, presenting a blank front to the urgent glances constantly being directed at him by father and daughter. Gina was disturbed. His face was unreadable, the dark deep-set eyes hooded, and she was increasingly afraid he was going to back George, and propose inaction until Susie was older.

Ross knew he couldn't do this, no matter how much he might sympathise with George's anguish. When in doubt, he reminded himself, not for the first time or the last, follow whatever line is in the patient's own best interest. About this he had no doubt. 'I do understand your hesitation,' he told George. 'The possibility of a transplant for any patient is daunting. A tremendous undertaking for patient and family, exactly as you say. But I'm bound to add that so much is changing today for young cystic fibrosis patients that for Susie to see them in London and possibly be put forward for a place on the transplant programme could easily turn out to be life-saving for her.'

'I know it might be.' George sounded grim. 'If that's indeed the case, the last thing I would want to do would be to hold her back. But neither do I intend passively to hand her over like a laboratory specimen for investigation to a remote London hospital, far from her family, if here at home we could succeed in keeping her ticking over quietly in the way she's used to, with her family round her. That's my dilemma. And my responsibility.'

Gina wanted to say that the responsibility was in fact hers, but she held her fire. This discusison was only a repeat of many she'd had already. The difference today was that Ross was present. For some extraordinary reason she couldn't understand she had great faith in his ability to make a breakthrough for Susie where time after time she herself had failed. Well, after all, she rationalised, nothing like an outsider to step in at the psychological moment and change the entire picture. So she kept her fingers crossed and said nothing whatever.

'You are naturally very fond of her, after all these years,' Ross was saying to George. 'But at sixteen, as you've just said, she's not a child any longer. Don't you think it may be possible that at this stage she might actually be able to cope with a London teaching hospital?'

'Possible. Yes, of course it's possible, but I don't like it. Could be I'm hopelessly overprotective and overanxious. Another possibility, I admit.'

'I did in fact meet Mortimer's senior chest consultant myself quite recently,' Ross said. 'It was over a cystic fibrosis patient of his, as it happens, and I have to say that, far from being obsessed with research and investigations, he was almost as uneasy as you about allowing anyone on the surgical side to get their hands on her.'

Gina's eyes were brilliant again. Behind them she was silently cheering Ross on, and applauding his technique. He seemed to know intuitively exactly how to handle her father.

'The patient was a young woman—older than Susie, in her early twenties, as far as I remember. Anyway, he finally decided he did want to get her on to Tom Rennison's list for heart-lung transplant, and what I must point out here, George, is that there's always going to be a heartrending shortage of organs for transplant. Getting patients on the list doesn't necessarily mean that there's going to be an organ in time to save them. So if Susie's going to need a transplant at some stage, the best thing would be to get her on to the list as soon as possible.'

George looked stricken. 'I'd overlooked that,' he said heavily. 'That does make a big difference, no getting away from it. But I still hate the thought of our little Susie being caught up in all that hullabulloo. That scene is more like TV medicine than real life. Horrible.'

'I know just what you mean.' Tread warily, Ross was warning himself. But fight on. This child needs London, and a transplant. Her lungs are terrible. 'But as far as the Mortimer's patient was concerned, you'd have no doubts, I'm sure. There was no other choice. And as it turned out, the transplant was not only successful and life-saving—no way could she have gone on more than a month or two without it—but truly life-enhancing, too. She's fully fit, and leading a normal life for the first time ever. She's recently got married—we all had invitations to the wedding, it was great — and there seems no reason why in a year or two she shouldn't be able to go ahead and start a family.'

George gave another enormous sigh. 'Ross, I can see you and Gina between you are going to wear me down, and I suppose I have to accept it, you must both be right about this. However, if you don't mind, *festina lente*, eh? Let's not rush at it.'

Gina decided the moment had come to step in again. 'There can be no question of that in any case, Dad,' she said, as gently as she knew how. 'Before anything is decided, Susie'd need to see them again at St Mark's, wouldn't she? That would be the next stage. How do you feel about me going ahead and discussing it with them?'

'Right. You do that.' Distress made him abrupt — he was still very worried, feeling that they might be doing the wrong thing for Susie. 'That's it for the present, then. Thanks for your time, both of you. I can't honestly say I feel the better for our talk, but we've covered the ground, haven't we? I'll think about what you've said. Make an effort, I suppose, to bring myself up to date in the way you two think I should. See you later.' He'd been striding down the corridor towards the entrance as he spoke, and in the car park they separated.

Ross, pleased and stimulated by his first morning, brewed coffee in his attic flat and ate the ham sandwich Betty Armstrong had left ready for him. Gina, in her own flat over the garage at Rose Bank, also brewed coffee and with it consumed yoghurt and an apple, followed by half a Yorkie bar, instead of the cigarette she was accustomed to — and infinitely preferred, she decided. This made her think about Ross again. Having him in the practice was going to be great — in one morning he'd transformed the outlook for Susie. Gina felt light-hearted, and suddenly the future was inviting, sparking brilliantly ahead.

Only George, wading solidly through the three delicious courses that Daphne considered the minimum she could provide for a light lunch, was heavy-hearted and thoroughly uneasy, pressured and uncertain. He wanted only to do the best he could for little Susie — but what was it?

CHAPTER FIVE

Ross grew accustomed to the new framework of his days. After an early session of exercises in his big bathroom, now stacked with his various pieces of apparatus, he went downstairs in the lift at nine o'clock for morning surgery. Coffee with the partners would usually follow, when they discussed the morning's patients, their visiting lists, admissions or discharges at Vicky's, and any worrying cases. Then, while the others drove off on their rounds, Ross went across to the little cottage hospital and saw each of the practice's patients, though this might often be his second visit of the day. He normally woke early, and he had discovered that he learnt a lot if he dropped in for a word with the night staff before they went off.

Around midday he would return to his flat and embark on another bout of exercises — bending, stretching, hanging from the bar, working out on the bicycle or the rowing machine. The more conscientious he was over his daily exercises, the less pain he endured, so he tried not to omit this second workout. When he'd completed it, he'd shower, have a long drink of apple juice, make coffee and eat whatever Betty provided for his lunch.

After lunch was admission time at Vicky's, and he'd go over to receive any new patient from the practice. Often, too, as the weeks went by, he would be asked to see new admissions by doctors from other practices in Northborough. He'd be introduced to the patients, examine them with their GP, and afterwards, in the office, go into the case histories with the other doctor, who'd already asked Ross to include these patients in his late-evening round.

'Of course,' he'd say. 'Glad to. I'll be here anyway — it's only a step.'

'It's twenty-minutes' drive for me — we live outside Northborough, in the downs.'

'No problem.'

'Many thanks. We always used to have an arrangement with the assistant in the Hurst practice to look in on our patients for us last thing, but then when they stopped living over the surgery opposite we didn't think we could go on expecting it. Sure you don't mind?'

'Not a bit. The more the merrier — and I'll be over here anyway.'

'In that case, if you're agreeable, we'll see about renewing the former arrangement — George will put you in the picture, I'm sure.'

George did. 'The word's gone round that you're available, and they want to use you. What they do is pay into a kitty according to the number of their patients in Vicky's each night, and at the end of the year our practice gets a fee for functioning as what basically is resident medical officer for Vicky's. Most of the patients are fairly straightforward and reasonably stable — if they aren't, refuse to take them on. All you're called on to do is to keep an eye on them. If they blow up, you summon their own doctor, meanwhile, of course, starting any emergency treatment you consider necessary.'

'I'll be glad to take it on. It'll add to the interest of the late round.'

'Fine. I'll sort out the finances with them and let you

know what we agree. I shan't allow them to get away with too mean a pittance, rely on me.'

Ross was disturbed. 'But George, I don't want this to add yet again to the demands on you. That's the last thing I had in mind. Can't we just leave the finances to the end of the year, or something like that?'

'Not to worry, Ross. This is a very minor chore. I'm chairman of our BMA branch anyway, so I can fit it in after a meeting. Nothing to it. And I like to get all ends neatly tied off, you know.'

Too right you do, Ross thought. It became clearer with every day he was in Northborough that George was not only overworked, but temperamentally incapable of doing anything about it.

Susie was another example of this. Theoretically he'd handed her care over to Gina, but he remained unable to let go. He didn't intend to be interfering, but he never even pretended to wait for Gina to consult him, just kept on coming up with suggestions about her management. Gina had duly made the outpatient appointment for Susie at St Mark's, and she'd spoken to the consultant there about the possibility of trying to get her on to the heart-lung transplant programme at the Central London Hospital.

'Before Susie goes for her appointment,' Gina remarked over coffee one morning, 'I was thinking perhaps I should talk to her parents about the plan, so that they can discuss it with Susie, before I actually say anything to her myself. I was thinking I'd ask them to come in during evening surgery. That way Mr Winter wouldn't need to take time off from work.'

'Good plan,' George agreed. 'We should talk to them both at length, explain the implications, what would be demanded of Susie — and of them, too.'

Warning bells rang in Ross's head. *We*?

Evidently the same bells had rung for Gina. 'No need for you to be involved, Dad,' she said briskly, green eyes snapping. 'I'll be able to cope with them at this stage all right. If it comes to the point where Susie is accepted for a transplant, I'll call you in and we can have a big family discussion then.'

'No, I need to be in on the discussion from the outset,' George told her firmly.

Gina surveyed the toes of her highly polished shoes, flexing one ankle, and obviously, Ross decided, counting to ten. He was amazed to experience a strong urge not merely to back her up to the hilt, but to lean forward and stroke the ravishing ankle in its gossamer stocking.

At the psychological moment James stepped in — a habit of his. 'Why not let Gina go ahead and deal with it at this stage?' he said to George. 'It seems to me the time for you to come in is when the patient herself as well as the family are ready to talk.'

'That's right,' Gina said quickly. 'You come in later on, Dad, and add your weight, and — and authority to our deliberations after Susie's been to St Mark's, and we have a better idea how we're placed.'

Ross spotted an escape route. 'I can't help wondering if it may not be premature to talk to the parents before the girl has been seen at St Mark's. The time for what amounts to a case conference is after that appointment, rather than before, don't you think?'

Gina was quick to grasp the opportunity he'd offered. 'I'm jumping the gun, you mean? You're right. We can wait until after Susie's been seen at St Mark's before we talk to anyone. That would be much more sensible. No need to stir them up if nothing's going to come of it.'

'That's the last thing any of us would want,' George said. 'We'll leave it for the present, then.'

'One less call to make,' Gina said cheerfully, and crossed through a line on her list. She swallowed the last of her coffee. 'I'll be on my way, then.'

'I must get over to Vicky's,' Ross said, and rose.

'I'll come with you,' James sat at once. 'I want to have a word with Katrine about her mother — I saw her yesterday.'

They walked together across the road, and James said 'Ross, I've been meaning to have a word. Mainly about George, but somewhere away from the surgery and its interruptions. Are you free for lunch today?'

'Absolutely.'

'Good. We'll have a bite and a quiet chat. One o'clock? I'll meet you back in the surgery.'

'I'll be there.'

'We can go to Chez Guillaume,' James said. 'We can walk there, so no parking problems, or anything like that to bother about.'

They set off past Vicky's, and a hundred yards further on turned into the High Street. 'It's not much to look at from the outside,' James said. 'Down in the basement there under Pine World, in fact.' Pine World confronted them with an array of chests, tables and chairs spread out over the pavement, and James dived into a narrow doorway and down a spiral staircase to a quarry-tiled basement. The walls were brick, the tables draped in black and white gingham squares, while the rush-seated chairs had obviously been provided by Pine World. Every blank wall sprouted a flourishing spider plant and its progeny. 'Cheap and cheerful, as you can see,' James commented. 'But the cooking's quite something. They do a set lunch, which is good value. You can have any two out of three courses, and

personally I usually go for the soup and then some sort
of salad or vegetable dish—don't like filling myself up
at midday and then having to fight stupor for half the
afternoon. And we have a meal fairly early in the
evening with the kids.'

'No, I don't like too much at midday,' Ross agreed.

'The soup seems to be carrot and orange with
coriander,' James said. 'I'll have that.'

'Me, too. Sounds intriguing.' Ross was studying the
menu. 'And then perhaps stuffed green pepper with
rosti and a green salad.'

'I'll join you there,' James said, and gave the order.
'Oh, and a glass each of your dry white wine.'

'Very good, sir.'

'I don't usually drink at lunch, but this is to celebrate
your joining the practice,' James said.

'I'll very happily drink to that—thanks.'

'Now to George. I caught your expression when he
was doing his best to take over young Susie again,
although he handed her care over to Gina nearly a
year ago. It's typical, I'm afraid. We try to ease his
workload by taking over his patients, but he just can't
let go—and now you've seen exactly what we're up
against when we aim to reduce his hours.'

'Yes. There've been all sorts of little pointers, too.
That wasn't the first by any means.'

'No. Well, there you are. At least you're here, and
he's stopped doing his late round at Vicky's. Between
us we ought to be able to handle him, even if it takes
a wee while, but I'm afraid it's going to be mainly up
to you and me. Amrit's a sweet girl, and she's always
ready to help George if she can, but she gives in to
him far too easily. Tact and the mollifying phrase are
her forte, and she lets George get away with too much
interference. Far too much. Gina's much tougher with

him, but then she's in a difficult position, and there's a limit to how far we can expect her to go in standing up to George.'

'She hasn't seemed to me to have much problem in asserting herself,' Ross said drily.

'No, but it stresses her, and she's got her mother's anxiety to cope with as well. You've met Daphne, haven't you?'

Ross nodded. 'A bundle of neuroses.'

'Exactly. Well-meaning, but panicky, and as obsessional about detail as George. Poor old George — he's doing his best in difficult circumstances. He's given up smoking, and he's trying to cut down on fat, when Daphne will let him.'

'He mentioned the smoking to me — said he'd been on twenty a day.'

'Afraid so. He and Gina both, and both supposed to have given it up, though I have my doubts as far as Gina is concerned. I've noticed a distinct whiff of tobacco from her in the surgery early in the morning and after lunch. I've been meaning to tackle her about it.'

'I'm afraid I beat you to it.' Ross pulled a face, and told James about the incident in the Rose and Crown. 'I handled it very badly, no getting away from it — I was pretty ashamed of myself afterwards.'

'You were absolutely right to slam into her. I'd have done the same.'

'Her smoking is an accepted problem, then?' Ross was startled to feel, instead of his previous irritation, a sudden uprush of compassion for the lovely and exasperating Gina, saddled with an addiction she couldn't handle, in addition to a problem father with angina and an over-anxious fusspot of a mother.

James nodded. 'However, that can wait. George is

today's worry. Now you're here and settled in I'm going to insist George cuts down on work still more. He's going to have to shed more patients—some of them on to you, if you agree. And that brings me to my next point. You've been finding out, I don't doubt, much more about your own capabilities, how much you're able to do at a stretch, for instance, and day after day. How's it been? And I want the truth, mind.'

'It's been OK. Mainly because I find I can pace myself. The long hours don't bother me in the least. As long as I can fit in my exercises before lunch and have a bit of a break then, I'm fine. However, if I'm to be any real use, and any real help with George, I need to take on home visits. Until I do I'm not pulling my weight.'

'In due course, I've no doubt you'll be able to. But don't push it. Slow and steady will be more use than trying too hard too soon, and then having to lie low and recuperate. I don't think you need attempt home visits just yet. After all, in the surgery, or in Vicky's, if you were on the blink, there'd be someone around to cope.'

'I'd like to give it a whirl. I don't think the patients would suffer.'

'I suppose you could at least try it out and see how you get on. You could start with some of George's old faithfuls, say, where we know exactly what the set-up is, and what the patient's going to need. You'd need a car, though.'

'That's fixed. Next week. I'm due to take delivery of a new Volvo. I'm having it specially adapted. As my legs are, to say the least, unreliable, I'm having an automatic with manual controls, special seating with extra springing and back support plus various fail-safe devices, extra signalling touch controls, telephone—

you name it, this car will have it. It'll probably brew up tea or coffee and make sandwiches, I shouldn't wonder, by the time they're through with it. Once I've got it I'll be adequately mobile for home visits.'

'You seem to have thought of everything, I must say. All the same, it won't be easy. So don't hesitate to let me know if there's a point — or a half-day, if you need it — when you want out. I'll cover for you, no problem.'

'I hope to be able to cope without demanding assistance,' Ross said stiffly.

'Now, Ross, don't start out by emulating George, for Pete's sake. One of the practice to watch and worry over is quite enough. The sooner you face the fact that you're not one-hundred-per-cent fit twenty-four hours a day, every day, the better for you and everyone else. You told me when we first met that you didn't want people watching out for you non-stop, as they were doing at the Central. The way to be free of that is always to ask for help when you need it, so that we can rely on that, and don't have to be on tenterhooks to make sure you're not in difficulties.'

'Point taken.' Ross smiled sardonically. 'You've caught me out. Secretly, I reckon, I'm still trying to kid myself that I *am* one-hundred-per-cent, if not a hundred and fifty. Pathetic, isn't it? But I used to be very fit, and I'm afraid I rather prided myself on it. I have to unlearn old attitudes. I have some sympathy with George, you know. Just like him, I don't find it easy.'

'A habit comes with practice. You must start confiding the state of your health routinely, that's what you must do. So remember I'll be listening. You're not finding the average day's work too demanding?'

'Not so far. One advantage about general practice is

that, taking the day as a whole, it's slower than surgery, and much more broken up. At present, I've easily been able to give myself gaps to rest, put my feet up, or do some limbering-up to flex my spine.'

'Useful, I see that. Though I don't altogether care for that word slow. Are you finding general practice slow and boring?'

'Do you find it slow and boring?'

'Never. Engrossing. But then it's my first choice.'

'It's dealing with people again, and it's clinical medicine. People are what I've been missing all these years—people, human beings with their muddled lives and problems, and their puzzling non-textbook conditions. It's the absence of people that's been bugging me, I suspect, more than the everlasting paperwork of management.'

'I agree completely. Medicine is people, morning, noon, and, far too often, night. Infuriating, maddening, impossible people. I'd miss them like hell if they weren't around.'

CHAPTER SIX

Ross went to bed that night blithely congratulating himself on how what he had told James was the exact truth. His health was holding up splendidly. He had tempted fate. Around two in the morning he woke with one of the worst bouts of pain he'd had to endure for months. Activity and exercise could sometimes lessen the pain, so that he need not take the drugs he'd been prescribed but loathed taking. He climbed reluctantly out of bed and walked unsteadily around the cold flat, trying to persuade his protesting legs to settle down. However, his muscles went on refusing to relax, and so, although he'd seldom felt less like energetic movement, he sat down on his exercise bicycle and pedalled vigorously.

He was exhausted before he started, but the instant he stopped pedalling, the cramps and spasms returned in full force. So what next? What he needed was warmth and gentle activity, and he wasn't getting it. The flat had no central heating, and though he'd switched on the wall fire high up in the bathroom, it was barely taking the edge off the chilly night air.

The obvious answer came to him. Opposite, on the other side of the road, was Vicky's. It would be warm there, and quietly busy. If he appeared, no one would think anything of it, and he'd soon warm up. He could check on one or two patients, have a word with those awake and in pain, and then relax over a hot drink — like all night staff, both sisters were apt to proffer Horlick's or Ovaltine on any excuse or none. He'd soon forget his own discomfort. Vicky's was the place to be, not this freezing bathroom.

He didn't like to wake the Armstrongs on the next floor by summoning the noisy old lift at this hour, so he set off down the stairs—step by uneasy step. This made his cramps and spasm worse. His legs didn't care for his chosen activity at all.

Too much, too soon, he told himself. And not for the first time, either. Would he never learn? However, here he was, halfway down the stairs. To go on would be more useful than to retrace his steps and climb up into the chilly flat again. He reached the hall, unlocked the front door and let himself out into the quiet moonlight.

The night was fresh and even more chilly, naturally, than the flat. His legs hated it, and he knew at once that he'd been every sort of idiot. He should have stayed in bed and taken his painkillers.

Across the road the subdued lights of Vicky's glimmered enticingly. He could be there in a minute or two, it would be gloriously warm, and he'd soon be over his problems. Jerkily, he set off across the road, but it wasn't easy, and the steps leading up to the porch proved hazardous. However, every muscle crying out, he managed it, though he almost fell into the hall with its one shaded lamp, and staggered a little wildly along until he could collapse into the chair by the unused reception desk. He'd been so intent on not falling over that it was only when he was safely seated that he remembered what his eyes had seen while he'd been forcing himself across the drive. It hadn't been empty. Gina's Jaguar stood there. She must be here.

His world turned upside down. He was elated, his pain forgotten. That maddening creature with her incredible eyes was here. Any moment she'd appear. They'd be together.

They were together now, this minute. A quick rush of feet along the corridor behind him, a voice throwing comments back to Abby, a murmur in reply.

'I'll look in before surgery and see how she's doing, all right? But I think she'll be quite OK now.'

She stopped dead, skidding in her tracks, and stared down at him, her eyes startled, enormous. She was wearing a calf-length black skirt, a black chiffon blouse, tucked and wide-sleeved, and distinctly rumpled and the worse for wear. She'd been working in it, no mistaking that. In one hand she carried her medical bag, in the other a glittery evening bag.

She'd been out somewhere. Who with? Ross seethed, and then, recollecting the notions, however outdated, of formal courtesy in which he'd been reared, he clambered, less elegantly than he would have wished, to his feet. 'Morning, Gina, Abby.' His body protested furiously at this unexpected demand, and he clenched his teeth against waves of agony.

'What on earth are you doing here?'

'Charming. Marvellous welcome you offer.' His lip curled, as his pain spoke for him. He would have called the words back if he'd known how. What he should have done was to tell her the truth, be straight-forward about why he was here in the small hours of the morning. She was a doctor and his colleague, he had only to give her the briefest of explanations and she'd understand completely. She'd pump painkiller into him and administer TLC, he was certain she would. And it would be great. But he couldn't do it. He was going to turn his back on it, walk away, keep his mouth shut. That was what he was going to do, he knew it. He disapproved, but he wasn't going to be able to stop himself.

'Learn to admit you're not always one-hundred-per-cent, that your health is impaired and you're going sometimes to need help.' He could hear James's voice clearly in his mind, and he agreed with every word.

But he couldn't do it. There she stood, fashionable and oh, so desirable, and he was quite unable to open his mouth and admit he felt awful. Instead, he glared into the disturbing green eyes and dared her to question him in any way about anything under the sun. Or, more appropriately, the moon.

The eyes scanned him, assessed him clinically. 'You're not well,' she said flatly.

Surprise, surprise. Your diagnostic flair is outstanding, Doctor. Somehow he managed not to throw these phrases at her—largely, though, because he was feeling so horrible, and needed to concentrate in order to remain upright, never mind coherent.

'What's wrong? Hadn't you better sit down?'

'I'm perfectly all right,' he lied through gritted teeth, standing four-square on his screaming legs.

'Of course you aren't.' She dismissed this idiocy out of hand. 'You're white, and you're sweating.' She took his pulse, which bounded wildly.

Hastily, Ross sat down, jerking his wrist away from her warm fingers. 'Just leave me alone, can't you? That's all I ask. I'll be perfectly all right.' Angry with himself, he had no understanding of the powerful antagonism that surged across from his taut frame.

Cut to the quick, Gina took a step back. She found herself, unusually for her, not knowing what on earth to do next. She had no idea how to handle him.

'Leave me alone, for crying out loud. There's absolutely nothing wrong that anyone can do anything about, and I'll handle it myself. Good grief, if I can't manage, and in any case I bloody can, Abby's here on the premises.'

So get lost, and fast, Gina Hurst. He hadn't spoken the words, but Gina knew that was what he meant. 'Up to you,' she snapped back, her voice brittle. 'If that's what you want, right. Goodnight.' Being spoken to like this by Ross, when he looked so ill, was so clearly in desperate need, was—for some inexplicable reason—almost reducing her to tears. She turned her back, the heels of her high strappy sandals clicked away down the hall, she let herself out, walked across to the Jaguar, started the engine and drove away.

What on earth could be the matter with her? Ross was ill—and in a bad temper, too. But he needed looking after.

Well, if he did, Abby was there, as he'd pointed out so offensively. Abby could look after him. Finish.

Ridiculous to be upset because he was ready to accept help from Abby but not from her. Forget it.

What she needed was a cigarette.

Since the fiasco in the Rose and Crown, Gina no longer carried the carton in her handbag. She *was* going to stop smoking. It was taking a little longer than expected, but she was going to stop.

Back in her own living-room, she found the carton, picked it up. And put it down again. She was going to stop, wasn't she?

She was going to stop now. Not next week, or next month. Now. She picked up the carton again, walked through to the kitchen with it and dropped it into the bin. That was the end of that. And she was never going to buy another twenty, either. Never.

She ran a bath, and lay in it thinking about Ross. He had looked so ill. Exhausted, too. She had wanted, she remembered with an unwelcome pang of anguish, she had longed to put her arms round him and make him well. The healing touch. Huh. Garbage. He didn't want her assistance. 'Leave me alone,' he'd said. The memory hurt as much as the reality had done, and this time there was no one to see how much she minded. She lay in the bath crying.

He wanted her as far away as possible. He must hate her.

So what if he did? It was her own fault, she'd brought it on herself; she'd simply have to live it down. It wasn't worth being miserable about. One of life's minor problems, no more. So why was she crying as if her heart was broken?

Well, because it was three in the morning, and she was tired. That was the explanation.

Over in the little office in Vicky's, Ross took one of his painkillers and a muscle relaxant, and drank the creamy Horlick's Abby had made. She'd also turned on the electric fire to supplement the already more than adequate central heating, and the small room was like an oven. His legs loved it, and the pain was already diminishing. He was warm and comfortable at last, cosseted and cared for, wrapped tenderly about with Abby's concern.

He'd been horrible to Gina. In hindsight his behaviour seemed demented. Why on earth hadn't he put her in the picture? Why make such a mountain out of it? They were both medically qualified, and they should be able to talk about the effects of his own injuries as easily as about the illness of a patient.

His ego was involved, that was why he hadn't told her. He had to recognise it. He was unable to admit to this sexy overpowering beauty that his body could let him down like this. Crazy. In the morning he had to pull himself together and apologise for his abruptness.

He drank the last of the Horlick's. Hardly any pain now. He'd better get himself back to his own flat before he dropped off to sleep here. He stood up cautiously.

All right. Steady as a rock.

He went in search of Abby, thanked her for the Horlick's, and told her he was off.

'Are you sure you're all right? I could easily come across the road with you — Staff would cover here.'

'I'm revived. Restored. OK — thanks to you. I'll see you tomorrow — sorry to have been such a nuisance.'

'Look after yourself, won't you, Ross? You did look quite poorly, you know. I think perhaps you should have taken your tablets much earlier.'

'You're dead right, I should have done. Anyway, I'm fine now. Goodnight, Abby — morning, I should say.' He went off fairly slowly, to be on the safe side. He managed the stairs, though it took him some time, let himself into the flat, and fell into bed, where he went out like a light, and knew nothing until his alarm woke him.

He felt heavy and disinclined to move, and sat on the side of the bed rubbing his hands through his dark hair, while his body protested that movement of any kind whatever was entirely alien to it. 'Come on, get cracking,' he told it. 'On your way.' He levered himself up, and trod across to the bathroom. He had time for a bath, and it would loosen him up as nothing else could do.

It did, and he felt better, went into the kitchen to make coffee and eat muesli. He was later than usual. No time for his exercises — five minutes on the bike, and the rest would have to wait. With any luck he'd be able to fit them in between coffee and his round at Vicky's.

He went down, in the lift this time, to the hall, where Betty, at the desk, gave him a frowning glance. 'Are you all right? You look absolutely exhausted.'

'Bad night, that's all. I'm all right really.'

'I'm sorry.'

'Thanks. Can't be helped.' He crossed the hall to the small room where he saw patients. Surgery this Thursday morning was busy, patients poured through steadily, and the last didn't leave until nearly eleven. By then Ross was feeling alert, and had almost forgotten his tiredness earlier. He decided to miss coffee, and instead get in a good bout of exercises before going over to Vicky's. 'I'll skip coffee this morning,' he told Betty as he passed her desk. 'Upstairs if you need me for anything.'

The telephone rang, and she nodded acknowledgement as she answered it. She was compiling visiting lists, which somehow were always completed by the end of surgery—in fact she usually took them in with the coffee. Today, though, they were mostly grabbed from her in the hall, for Ross was not the only one to miss coffee; everyone was in a rush and on the move.

Amrit was the first off. She wanted to get ahead with her visits, as she was due, she reminded Betty, at a Townswomen's Guild luncheon at the Rose and Crown, where she had to give a talk on 'Mother and Working Doctor'. In honour of the townswomen, she was wearing a sari, and looking fabulous, as Betty told her.

Her departure was quickly followed by Gina's, called out to a delivery on the outskirts of the practice, a lone caravan at the end of a farm track in the downs, she explained to Betty as she rushed by. 'This dippy girl has been living there alone, wouldn't you know, saying nothing to anyone, and she's gone into labour with no preparations whatever — the farmer's wife rang the midwife, who's a friend of hers. I don't know how long this is going to take, or how far advanced she is, but I could easily be held up until early afternoon. I'll be in touch if I can, but I'll have to leave the car at the farm, so I may not get a chance to ring in — or, of course, I may. But to be on the safe side, check my list, would you, and unload anyone really urgent on to one of the others. Didn't you say Miss Oliver rang? Better get someone to do that for me, anyway, as soon as poss. You know how she panics.'

Betty knew only too well. Miss Oliver was a regular, though the patient was not herself but her mother, who, although in her nineties, had practically nothing wrong with her. Miss Oliver, though, herself in her late sixties, was a worrier, and when her mother, who enjoyed the stimulus and attention of a visit from the doctor, told her daughter to ring the surgery and ask for a call, Miss Oliver invariably leapt to the conclusion that her aged parent was about to depart from this world. The problem for the Hurst practice was that one day, inevitably, Miss Oliver was going to be right in this assumption. Both Gina and Betty, though, could be reasonably confident that today was not the day. 'Don't worry, I'll cope with her,' Betty said cheerfully, with not a glimpse of how wrong she would be proved to be.

Since Thursday was James's day off, only George remained for coffee, and Betty took it in to him, with his own list and Gina's, and told him what had happened.

'Oh, yes,' he said, 'I'll do the Olivers, sure. First call, it had better be, I suppose, though I don't for a

minute expect there's a thing wrong with the old dear.
Cross her off Gina's list, though. Anyone else urgent?'

'Only an asthmatic child Gina went out to last night
and admitted to Vicky's. She saw her before surgery,
but she'd intended to pop over and see her again
before she went on her round—I can ask Ross to
check on her, though.'

'Do that. The rest of this lot can wait for Gina this
afternoon.'

The telephone in the hall rang again, and Betty went
to answer it. Miss Oliver, asking why her mother had
not yet been visited.

Raising her eyes towards the ceiling, Betty explained
that morning surgery had only just finished. Yes, she
had given Dr Hurst the message. Yes, Dr Hurst did
know about it.

'Then where is she, pray? I rang three hours ago, at
a quarter past eight. Before I got breakfast. Surely she
could have been here by now?'

'I'm afraid Dr Hurst has been called away to an
urgent case,' Betty said with some relish. It was a
mistake.

'Are you telling me my mother is *not* urgent? Isn't
she entitled to some consideration? At her age?'

'Well, you see, Miss Oliver, the other call was from
the midwife, and I'm afraid it's no use expecting babies
to wait for anyone, is it?'

Since Miss Oliver could think of no satisfactory
answer, she replied in a tone of outrage, 'Disgraceful.
Quite disgraceful.'

'Before she left, Dr Hurst told me to ask Dr Hurst
senior to call on your mother, Miss Oliver. I've just
given him the message, and I'm sure he'll be along as
soon as he possibly can.' Betty was dulcet, though she
was pulling hideous faces at the telephone.

Far from being mollified, Miss Oliver was even more infuriated. 'You mean you've only just told him? I find that extremely casual, to say the least. After all, I rang you before breakfast, and now it's nearly lunchtime, and you've only just passed the message on. My mother could be dead by now.'

Firmly repressing a wicked temptation to say, 'But she isn't, is she?' Betty, with a face like thunder, and an edge to her voice, said, 'We had a heavy surgery this morning, Miss Oliver, and the doctors have only just been able to leave on their visits. I'm sure Dr Hurst will be along to see your mother quite soon.'

'I don't suppose he's even left,' Miss Oliver snapped, with unerring accuracy. 'Has he? Can you honestly assure me he's on his way?'

Betty, of course, couldn't. 'I'm not sure, Miss Oliver, I'm afraid,' she said weakly. 'He might still be over at the cottage hospital. I —— '

'Nothing but excuses. It's always the same. None of you bothers about elderly people. We count for nothing, we're simply has-beens. No one over sixty amounts to a row of beans. When I was a girl it was different. We respected our grandparents. No one has any respect these days, and you think we none of us count, we can await your convenience.'

This was going a bit far, even for Miss Oliver on a bad day, Betty thought. She swallowed her fury, and tried to be calming. 'Of course Dr Hurst doesn't think anything like that, Miss Oliver. None of us does,' she said soothingly. 'We are all hoping your mother will continue on in good health right through her nineties and make a hundred. And I expect she will, you know.'

'Not if the doctor can't be bothered to visit her when I ask,' Miss Oliver retorted nastily.

Betty swallowed. This had got thoroughly out of hand, she realised. She needed assistance. And Miss Oliver needed the senior partner's touch. 'Ah,' she exclaimed brightly. 'There *is* Dr Hurst senior. Hold on a moment, Miss Oliver, will you, while I just have a word with him?'

'I've got Miss Oliver on the line again, I'm afraid, in one of her states. Perhaps if you had a word with her? Even if just to reassure her that you really are on your way? She seems to be working herself up into a terrific tizzy. She says she rang at a quarter past eight to ask for a visit, no one's been, it's nearly lunchtime, it's a disgrace, and so on. And on.'

'Was the first call at eight-fifteen?'

'Oh, yes, it was. But she didn't say anything then about it being urgent, simply said could she have a visit this morning, her mother wanted to see Dr Hurst. Now she's saying she and her mother don't count, because they're old, they can await our convenience, and so on. There's no respect, I'm afraid.' Betty pulled a face.

It was George's turn to raise his eyes towards the ceiling. 'I'll have a word with her,' he said, 'try to pacify her before she goes pop. Put her through, Betty.'

Betty went back and transferred Miss Oliver, and then began her routine tidying of the consulting rooms, to leave them ready for the afternoon appointments. She was back at her desk filing cards and waiting to catch Ross to tell him about the asthmatic in Vicky's, when George's buzzer sounded, and the light above his door began flashing. This was the signal to send in the next patient, but what on earth did it mean now, at this hour of the morning? Perhaps there was a short somewhere. She'd have to send for the electrician, get

it fixed in time for evening surgery. What a pest. Or
could George still be there? Did he want something?

She walked across, opened the door of his room,
and looked in.

He had not left. He was lying on the floor by his
desk. His colour was horrible.

She rushed across the room, knelt down by him.

'Betty,' he said at once. 'Good girl. Get —— ' he was
breathless ' — get one — of the doctors. Reckon I'm —
coronary. If you can't — get doctor, get Katrine over.
Not ambulance, Betty. Not St Mark's. But fast. OK?'

'I'll be able to catch Ross, I'm sure.' Betty stood up,
and then hastily knelt down again. 'George, she said
urgently. 'Your Trinitrate?'

'Not working.'

'I'll get Ross.'

Back in the hall, Betty rang the top flat, and Ross
answered at once, to her immense relief. 'Can you
come down *stat*? George says he's having a coronary,
and he looks awful.'

'On my way.'

Almost immediately Betty heard the old lift begin
its clanking descent, and she was standing by it, ready
to open the outer door as the ancient cage shuddered
to a halt. Ross, in jeans and trainers and a sweat shirt,
and carrying his medical bag, shot out, demanding,
'Where is he?'

'In his room,' Betty said. 'I'll deal with the lift.' The
final sentence was in fact addressed to his back, and
then he had vanished into George's room. Betty shut
the heavy lift doors, and joined him.

He was kneeling by George's side behind the desk.
He had pulled off George's tie — she saw it lying on
the floor — opened his shirt and had his hand against

the side of his neck, feeling the pulse. George himself was now a nasty mauve colour.

'He does still have a pulse,' Ross commented. 'Do you happen to know if he's had his Trinitrate?'

'I asked. It wasn't working, he said.'

George opened his eyes, took in Ross's presence. 'Sorry,' he said. 'Nuisance.'

'Not to worry. You'll be all right,' Ross said firmly. 'Between us we'll make sure of that.'

George moved his head restlessly. 'Painful,' he said. 'Very. Like they say. And won't stop. Listen. Vicky's, if you have to. No further.'

'I'll see to it. Meanwhile I'll do something about the pain, how'll that be? You'll feel a bit better, and we can go ahead and treat you.' He stood up, made Betty gasp as he cleared a space for his bag on George's desk by the simple method of sweeping the trays and prescription pads to the floor, opened up his case, took out a syringe and an ampoule, all the while talking, first to George — 'Better in a minute now,' he said to him — and then to Betty. 'Bring the electrocardiograph over here, will you, and plug it in at the wall for me?'

Betty did this, and saw that Ross was injecting George with whatever it was he'd taken out of his case. Morphia? Adrenaline? She had no chance to ask him, he was issuing further instructions to her.

'Ring across to Vicky's and ask Katrine to get over here at the gallop. Tell her what's happened.' He turned to the desk and scribbled something. 'Tell her to bring this,' he said.

This surprised Betty — why didn't he simply tell her?

'Shut the door behind you,' he added.

This surprised her even more, though when she read what he'd written down she understood at once. He didn't want George to realise what he wanted Katrine to do.

She shut the door behind her, went to her desk and dialled.

'Queen Victoria's. Sister Fremantle.'

'Betty here, from the Hurst surgery opposite. Dr Hurst is having a coronary. Dr Nicholson is with him, and he says can you come over *stat*, and bring your defibrillator with you.'

'With you as fast as I can make it.'

Betty went down the hall, opened the front door and fastened it back, and then returned to George's room. 'She's on her way,' she told Ross, who had a mask over George's face and was giving him oxygen. 'I've left the front door open for her.'

'Good. Where's Gina?'

'Out on a midder at the end of a farm track. Probably unreachable — she said she'd have to leave her car at the farm, she thought.'

'Oh, big deal. Ring James, then, see if he can drop everything and come over.'

Betty went back into the hall, and dialled the familiar number. While she was doing this, there was a rapid crunching on the gravel outside, a rush of feet on the steps, and Katrine came pounding in. 'There,' Betty said, gesturing towards George's room, and Katrine shot inside, carrying the defibrillator in its case.

Dr Black's telephone was answered by his wife, Meg.

'Surgery here. Is James about?' Betty asked. 'It's a bit urgent.'

'Sorry. He's out playing golf. Anything I can do?'

'Ross thinks George is having a coronary. He's with

him, and Katrine's just arrived from Vicky's, but Ross said to try and get James. Gina's out at a midder.'

'I'll ring the golf club and make them go out and find him. I'll be in touch.'

Betty went back into George's room, where she found that though they hadn't moved him from the floor, Ross and Katrine had made him more comfortable. There was a cushion under his head, and his feet were resting on his own desk chair, on another cushion, instead of against the side of the desk, as they'd been when she first found him. He was covered by the blanket from the examination couch, and attached to his own electrocardiograph machine. The defibrillator was ready but not in use. He was still getting oxygen, and his colour was perhaps not quite so frightful.

Katrine was on the point of departure, it seemed. 'I'll bring a trolley over, then,' she said. 'Plus anything else I happen to think of, and tell them to have the resuscitation room ready.' The door shut behind her.

'Any luck with James?' Ross asked.

'On the golf course, wouldn't you know? Meg's going to ring them and make them find him and send him here, but if you ask me all that could easily take half an hour minimum.'

'You're right, it could. Easily. Better try Amrit, see if you can winkle her out of that Rose and Crown lunch — unless she's actually on her feet speaking, that is. Anyway, leave a message for her.'

'Right. Do you think I ought to ring Daphne and get her to come over?' Betty asked anxiously.

Ross scowled at her, and Betty was taken aback. Daphne surely had a right to be told, so that she could come straight over? Then she realised her words had worried George. She hadn't realised he was fully conscious, but he'd heard her, and now his eyes were wide open and he was muttering behind the mask.

Ross leant down. 'What was that?'

'Not to come here. Daph. Get Meg — go to her.'

'Don't worry. I'll see to it. Leave it for now, Betty,' Ross told her. 'Remind me, and I'll deal with it later.'

Betty returned to the hall, feeling guilty and upset. She'd wanted only to help, but all she seemed to have achieved was to make things worse.

The telephone rang, and she leapt on it, hoping for Meg or James. But it was only someone asking about surgery times, and then wanting to make an appointment. Betty entered it in the book, wondered briefly who, if anyone, would be taking surgery that evening, and began looking up the number of the Rose and Crown.

There was a crunching on the gravel again, heralding Katrine's return with the trolley. Betty helped her up the steps with it, and then they came trundling down the hall and into George's room.

CHAPTER SEVEN

Two hours later, George was in Vicky's, attached to the monitor in the little ward alongside the resuscitation room, with the defibrillator, oxygen and a ventilator at the ready. James and Ross were standing over him. Katrine, who had been with them to settle him in, had just departed to her office to organise a belated — it was coming up for three o'clock in the afternoon — sandwich lunch for everyone.

'We can work out over our sandwiches exactly how we're going to run the practice as well as look after George, for the coming weekend, at any rate. For the next twenty-four hours our priority is going to be for one of us to be here to keep an eye on him,' James was saying. 'Luckily, we always have a pool of nurses available on Vicky's books only too glad to take on a stint of private nursing when required. But to start with I'd be easier in my mind if one of us was standing by uninterrupted — at least Amrit must be clear of her townswomen by now, and Betty will be bound to send her straight across here.' He grinned briefly. 'And unlike the rest of us, she'll be full of good nourishing food, too, so she can come and stay here while we eat. If you'd just hang on for five minutes or so, I'll brief her and then she can take your place. You've had three hours on the go without a break. So how are you feeling yourself?'

'I'm fine, thanks. No untoward symptoms.'

'Good. Start by taking the weight off your feet now — sit down at the end of the bed, put your feet up on the bed rail, and watch George and the monitor. Unless anything changes, I forbid you to do more.'

'That seems the height of slackness.'

'Take any rest you can, while you can. What we need is to have you beavering away in rude health. Sit.'

'Just as you say, Doctor,' Ross assured him, dark eyes glinting.

'Stick to that, m'lad, and you can't go wrong. Meanwhile, if you need me, I'll be in Katrine's office.'

Amrit Patel, it turned out, was there before him, and so, while coffee filtered on the side table, James brought her up to date.

Outside the small ward, Gina, agony in her wide green eyes, her face white and strained, paused momentarily to collect herself. Calling in at Rose Bank to wash and change after delivering a healthy eight-pound baby boy and attending to his shattered teenage mother, she had found Meg with Daphne, and been given the news about her father, by then already in Vicky's. Now, however panicky she felt inwardly, she knew she must radiate calm and confidence, for George's sake. She had never felt less confident. She took several slow, steadying breaths, opened the door very quietly, and stepped cautiously in.

The first sight to meet her eyes was Ross, sitting at the foot of George's bed, his chair tipped back at a dangerous angle, watching the monitor and George alternately. For some reason she didn't stop to work out, seeing him made her feel better at once.

Her father was asleep. He wasn't too bad a colour — in fact he looked a lot better than her imagination had painted him — he was on a drip, and the tracing on the monitor was not too horrific, either. Relief swept through her, and suddenly she wanted to burst into tears. She had made it in time. She was here, on the spot. She'd keep him alive, somehow pour her own vigorous health into him.

Ross ached for her. The poor love. Exhausted, pale, still bloodstained—once she'd heard the news, he saw, she'd simply rushed straight to Vicky's. She as much as George needed cherishing—as if she'd let him, he thought wryly. She'd reject any form of support for herself out of hand. 'He's not doing at all badly,' he said gently. 'James will have told you——'

'I haven't seen him. I came straight here when I heard.'

'Well, then, to start with how he is now, as of this minute. As you can see, the tracing isn't marvellous, there's this raised ST segment, but it's a good deal better than it was two hours back, and his pulse is much stronger——'

The door opened, and James came in, accompanied by Amrit, still in her best sari.

'Ah, here you are, Gina,' he said. 'Good. Amrit is going to take over here; you'd better go into Katrine's office and Ross can bring you up to date on how George is doing. I have to go over to see Mrs Oliver, she hasn't been seen yet, but I shouldn't be long. Meanwhile—I don't suppose you've had any food— there are coffee and sandwiches in the office, and you can both eat while Ross tells you what's been happening.'

Gina opened her mouth to explain that she was going nowhere. She was staying here, in this room, with her father. But she shut it again immediately. Not to panic, she reminded herself. Not to make scenes, either. And James was absolutely right. She'd be far more use when she'd heard the whole story, and had something to eat. Anyway, Ross would obviously be able to tell her more about George's condition over in the office, rather than standing here by his bed. And at least she'd now seen him for herself, with her own eyes. With a sigh, she turned and followed Ross along the corridor and into the office, fragrant with the coffee Katrine was pouring. A plate piled high with sandwiches occupied the centre of her desk. Gina felt faintly better, took a sandwich hungrily, bit into it and settled down to listen while Ross told her about George.

'Thank God you were there on the spot, Ross,' she said at last. 'Otherwise he might not have made it, I can see that.' She gave him a brilliant, tragic look from the enormous green eyes, set in a pale and shadowed face from which all make-up had long vanished.

Ross thought he'd never seen her more beautiful, and he yearned to be able to take her into his arms, hold her close, kiss her pain away and assure her that everything was going to be all right, rely on him. Unfortunately, as both of them knew only too well, this was in no way the case.

'The next twenty-four hours are going to be critical,' she said.

Ross agreed, passed her the sandwiches, refilled her coffee-cup, and launched into a slightly over-optimistic assessment of George's chances.

James returned, remarking that Mrs Oliver was fairly hale and hearty, and much more concerned now about George's health than her own. 'So back to George himself. What I suggest is that we arrange for one of us to be with him right through — say up to this time tomorrow, at least. We can think about extra nursing care after that. To begin with we'll look after him ourselves. There are four of us, so it will hardly be beyond our capacity—we'll only need to cover six hours each, on top of our usual routine.'

'I can do far more than six hours,' Gina told him. 'I'd like to be with him as much as I possibly can. What I'd prefer is for someone to take over my visits while I stay here with Dad.'

James vetoed this without hesitation. 'Sorry, Gina, it's not on. You're exhausted already, for one thing, which Amrit and I aren't. She's been demolishing a huge lunch and talking to the townswomen, and I've been playing golf. We're fresh. And then you have your mother to look after. After all, inevitably, you're going to be her first line of support. Meg's been at Rose Bank more or less since it happened, but it's you Daphne really needs.'

'Meg's been marvellous,' Gina said. 'It's only because she said she could stay with Ma that I came straight over here.'

'Of course that would be your first thought,' Ross said at once, longing still to be in a position to comfort her as if she were an anguished child.

Gina was unappreciative. She needed no one's support. First James, and now Ross, were trying to treat her like a child instead of a professional colleague. They were trying to protect her from reality, forgetting that she was as highly qualified as they were, if not more. They were behaving as if she was some patient's over-anxious relative.

This was at once underlined by James. 'Now you've seen how he is,' he said in his most warm and comforting tones, 'I think you should go straight home. Reassure your mother, bring her up to date, tell her George isn't at death's door—he's stable and he's not doing badly at all. You can also——' his tone changed and became that of the brisk senior colleague she'd been missing '—have a wash and change before evening surgery.' He gave her the sort of look pundits on ward rounds directed at dishevelled juniors.

Suddenly Gina realised what a mess she must look, and the realisation was oddly calming. She must wash and change, of course she must. James was right. And talk to her mother, too. A small series of mundane jobs lay ahead, and the future seemed less horrific. 'Yes,' she said quickly. 'I'll fit that in first of all. No problem.'

Always a firm believer in the use of accustomed routines to defuse anxiety, James talked determinedly on. 'What we have to think about next, and we may as well get it settled while you're here, is the rota for looking after George. You'll want to be with your mother tonight, so that leaves the night watch to be shared between Ross and me, then——'

'No. No, I'm sorry, Jamie, but it's simply not on.' Enough was enough. She was simply not going to agree to stay at home in bed while others saw her father through his most critical hours. She'd stay with him herself. Anything else was unthinkable. 'I'll stay with him myself tonight,' she said, with what she intended to be unshakeable firmness and authority, but which instead came quavering out with an ominous wobble, accompanied, too, not by the cool stare she'd planned, but by a melting appeal from suspiciously damp green eyes. 'I am,' she added tremulously, 'absolutely determined about this, Jamie. I'm not going to budge an inch.' She blew her nose hastily, furious with herself for displaying so much emotion.

It worked, though. James capitulated. 'If you're sure it's what you really want, then so be it. But if you change your mind, remember I'm ready to take over at any time.'

'I shan't change my mind.' She was crisp, in control again.

Back to the old Gina, Ross saw. One of her fast recoveries. That's my girl, he applauded inwardly. Never down for long. Up and at 'em.

'How about if you take over here at midnight, then?' James suggested. 'Go home now, see your mother, fit in a few visits if you can before doing surgery, then go off until midnight. Have a quick kip. I'll take over any outstanding visits from you, Ross will do his round here, and Amrit can stay with George until surgery. She can also take over your midder — better brief her. It's my day off, so I'm free to stay here with George while you all do surgery. In fact, I may as well stay until you take over at midnight. How does that strike you?'

'Terrific, Jamie, thank you. Do you want to go over my list now?'

'Not a bad idea,' James agreed at once, rightly assuming that Gina would find it a calming activity.

The rest of the day, to everyone's relief — not to mention amazement — went as planned. George remained stable, his tracing springing no nasty surprises. James sat with him from just before six onwards, except for a supper break when he dashed home while Ross relieved him. After this the two of them examined George together.

'Continuing the slow but steady improvement, I think we may dare to say,' James commented finally. 'Early days, though.' He looked at his watch. 'I'm expecting Kenneth Gray — he said he'd try to pop over between nine and ten. He's the cardiologist at St Mark's George has been seeing. I rang him to let him know what had happened.'

'A consultant on tap — that's a relief.'

'I'll say. I can't tell you how thankful I am to know he's on his way. We can do with him. It's a mercy you were on hand earlier, though. Because Gina was quite right. If you hadn't been on the spot, I don't reckon George would be with us now. There was me out on the golf course, Gina unobtainable at the end of a farm track in the downs, and even Amrit at the Rose and Crown could hardly have reached him in under twenty minutes — it could easily have been too late. Unless Betty had managed to catch someone from one of the other practices over in Vicky's at the crucial moment, we could have lost him. However, I want to talk about you now, not George. It's been a long hard day for you, and you've had hours of standing. How are you feeling?'

'I'm fine. Rather pleased with myself, if anything. It's been the most prolonged spell of uninterrupted work I've been involved in, and all my bits of jiggery pokery seem to have stood up to it OK. Once you were on the scene, of course, I eased up a bit, and I was able to sit down on and off. Since we've had George over here, I've been able to pace myself. I took the round here fairly slowly, I can tell you, and sat about on patients' beds in a way I wouldn't have dreamt of in the past.'

'Go off now, anyway, and get your head down. You're certainly entitled to.'

'I'll do my round, and then I'll be off.'

However, he was in fact writing up the day book in the office when Kenneth Gray walked in, so it was Ross who took him through to George's room. James immediately asked Ross to stay on, while Kenneth Gray went over George, heard their detailed report on the day's events, and assessed the situation. Kenneth, to the relief of both James and Ross, agreed

that at present the best place for George was undoubtedly Vicky's.

'He'll be happier here than anywhere else, we all,
know that, and you've obviously worked out a splendid
system of continuing care for the next twenty-four
hours. It would be a mistake to disturb him,' he said.
'I can pop over again tomorrow evening and have
another look at him—we can reconsider our plans
then, if we need to, but with any luck we shouldn't
have to.'

James saw Kenneth off, and rejoined Ross in
George's room. They'd hardly begun to discuss
Kenneth's comments and suggestions when Gina and
her mother arrived.

Daphne was pale and wan, but she seemed to have
herself under tight control, and there were no tears.
She greeted James with a hug and a kiss, shook hands
with Ross, and only then enquired, 'How is my darling
old thing, Jamie? Gina keeps telling me he's doing
well, and we've nothing to despair about.'

'You can see for yourself, Daphne, he's a good
colour, and he's sleeping peacefully. We've had
Kenneth Gray here, he's only just left, and he was
really quite pleased with him. So you can relax, though
I know it's hard.'

'Kenneth Gray's been to see Dad?' Gina's face lit
up.

'Yes. I rang him to tell him what had happened, and
he came over as soon as he could and spent over an
hour here.'

'How super of him. Oh, I do wish I'd been here
too.' Gina felt angry with herself for not having been
on the spot. She ought to have been there, she knew.

'Ross was here with me, and all three of us checked
George over very thoroughly.' James intended to be

reassuring, but succeeded only in making Gina feel neglectful, the only absentee. 'Anyway, Kenneth's coming over again tomorrow evening, bless him, to see how George is coming along, so you can talk to him then.'

'Tomorrow?' Gina was taken aback. 'But I assumed provided he was fit enough to move, of course, we'd be transferring him to St Mark's coronary intensive care first thing tomorrow morning.'

'I hope we won't need to do that at all, if all goes well,' James said firmly. He'd have to have it out, he saw, here and now. Not the time or the place he'd have chosen, but at least he had Ross to back him up. 'George was quite explicit, you know. He told both Ross and me that he wanted to stay here in Vicky's and not be moved to St Mark's. But we can discuss all this after Kenneth's been again tomorrow.'

Gina had been counting on getting her father into what she thought of as the safe environment of St Mark's intensive care, where state-of-the-art technology would be on tap, and George's care become the responsibility of highly qualified seniors. Cut off from the facilities and pundits of Mortimer's, with her father's life hanging in the balance, she was feeling very junior and very frightened. Though normally she had a high respect for James's skill as a clinician, she was simply too terrified to take this into account. It was clear, though, that any decision about moving George would have to be deferred until Kenneth Gray's next visit. 'I suppose we'll have to wait until he's been, then,' she agreed unwillingly. 'I do wish I'd been able to see him myself and put it to him, though.' She frowned, more from worry than disapproval.

Her mother, though, didn't see it like that. Her daughter was being difficult, she considered. 'Gina, dear,' she said, embarrassment plain—she thought her daughter had spoken out of turn—'of course we can trust James and Dr Gray to decide what's best for George.' To her, Gina was not so much the former registrar from the professorial medical unit at Mortimer's as a small and recalcitrant child.

James's mouth twitched. 'We'll talk about it in the morning,' he said, at that moment experiencing a good deal of sympathy for Gina, so unceremoniously reduced to the status of ignorant offspring speaking out of turn. 'There's no more to be done tonight. I'll drive you home, Daphne. Meg is definitely going to stay with you overnight, that's settled.'

In a few minutes they had gone, and Gina turned to Ross. He had been with George from the outset—most of her father's history since that morning, she'd seen for herself, was recorded in Ross's angular writing. They were comprehensive impeccable notes, and given that she hadn't been able to be with George herself, Ross's care had undoubtedly been life-saving. 'If you wouldn't mind telling me exactly what transpired with Kenneth, I'd be immensely grateful,' she said. Ross, she noticed as she turned to face him, showed clear signs of having been on duty far too long. He was grey with exhaustion, and she was to her amazement struck to the heart with a new and separate pain.

He showed no other sign of fatigue, though, moving over to the monitor, and starting to discuss the tracing now and as it had been earlier, and Kenneth's interpretation. This took some time, and Gina was as fascinated and absorbed as if she'd been back at Mortimer's. They went on to review the cardiologist's examination of her father, together with his findings, his opinion as to the outlook, and the lines of treatment he was advocating.

Ross was staring down at George, sleeping quietly, his breathing regular. 'With any reasonable luck, you know, he's going to make it, this time round,' he said. 'Kenneth certainly thinks so.' He gave Gina his sudden transforming smile. 'And seeing him now, I feel even more sure of it. He's so different from twelve hours ago when Betty called me down. I feel it in my bones, he's over it and he's going to come through.'

Gina wanted to hug him, and then dance round the room singing. Instead she heaved a huge sigh, and passed straight on to her next worry. 'The trouble is,' she pointed out, 'he ought not to be here in Vicky's at all. Not in this wretched little room with only us to look after him. I can't imagine what Kenneth can be thinking of. Dad ought to be in St Mark's.'

'Why?' Ross demanded.

'*Why*?' Anguished green eyes stared back at him. 'Surely it's obvious. For one thing, there'd be fully trained intensive care staff, a cardiac resuscitation team at the end of a bleep, plus X-ray and laboratory back-up. Not just you and me and James, however much we care.'

'Are you quite sure you want him moved for his own good, rather than just for your own peace of mind? To shift the responsibility?' The question was hard, but Ross's eyes were loaded with understanding and compassion.

'Of course I'd be tremendously relieved if he wasn't totally dependent on the few of us,' she admitted. 'But that's not the main reason. Surely you agree with me, they have the proper facilities and we don't.'

'But does George actually need those facilities? Are they of any importance at this stage? Don't you think moving him from his own familiar hospital, surrounded by trained people he knows and trusts, might be the worst possible action? Kenneth thinks so. And to transfer him to St Mark's in an ambulance, half an hour jolting along the road, then on to a trolley in reception, the glare of strip lighting, clatter bang crash all round, over to the lifts, manoeuvring the trolley in and out again, along to Intensive Care, being settled in, linked up to monitors and drips all over again, all this against the usual non-stop activity you get in Intensive Care — flashing lights, staff coming and going, telephones shrilling, and someone in the next bed very likely dying, too. Not good, you know. And hardly an improvement, I'd have thought, over staying quietly here with us.'

'All that's perfectly true, of course. I accept that. From that point of view staying here is familiar and unstressing, I agree absolutely. But we have no path lab on site, and only our portable X-ray, and the radiologist looking in once a day. Surely——'

'Gina, you must know as well as I do, most coronary patients, once they've stabilised, actually do better in their own homes than anywhere else.' He broke off. Enough was enough, he reminded himself. Gina had the long night watch ahead, and already she was not only worn out, but, it seemed, in a state of near-panic.

She sighed. 'Anyway,' she told him, 'no matter what I may or may not think, he's jolly well staying here until Kenneth comes again. What I have to do now is simply be with him and look after him, instead of carrying on wildly about possibilities that may never arise. I'll shut up and try to transform myself into a truly competent intensive care team, and——'

'But Gina, for Pete's sake, you don't have to try, that's exactly what you are. In fact, you're much more.

What you need is more confidence in yourself, that's all. For crying out loud, what patient in Intensive Care has the full and undivided attention of one teaching hospital registrar at his bedside throughout the entire night?'

She shot him a startled look. 'If you put it like that,' she said slowly, 'I suppose he isn't doing too badly.'

It was all up to her, though. And the prospect continued to terrify her.

Nonsense. She could cope. Of course she could. Ross was right. She, Gina Hurst, MD, MRCP, had precisely one patient to care for, until morning. That was all. There would be no other calls on her, no need to tear around, dividing herself between too many patients in too many different wards, relying on unfamiliar agency staff when she wasn't on the ward herself. Even so, she had never felt more lonely, and she longed as she'd never done before for a hand to cling to. Yet even Ross was going, though he said he'd be within reach if she needed a pair of hands. He'd decided to sleep here in Vicky's, he told her, he'd be along the corridor in the rest room if she wanted him. 'Any time. Don't hesitate.'

'Thanks. I'll remember — though I'll try not to have to call you. Night.'

'Night, Gina.'

The door shut behind him. Gina stood in the small room, alone with her father at last. Just as she'd insisted so fiercely. James hadn't wanted her to take this on, though he'd given in, allowed her to have her way, because he'd seen how much it had mattered to her. But he hadn't liked it. He'd been against it.

And he'd been right. She wasn't up to it.

Ross. Ross was here, just along the corridor. He was staying here all night. He was the support she'd been searching for. Right through to her bones she was sure of this. He could be relied on until hell froze.

She must be out of her mind. She was certainly going right over the top. This was melodrama. She was here in her own familiar local cottage hospital, any number of people within easy reach, and with just one single patient to watch over, recovering nicely from a minor coronary episode — that was how she would have seen it at Mortimer's. She was used to standing on her own two feet, making decisions for herself and others, carrying them out. She'd never looked anxiously around for support before, never longed for a shoulder to lean on. Why now?

She'd never before had to be responsible for her own father's life or death.

And she wasn't now, she reminded herself again. There was not only Ross, there was Abby, both only a step away along the corridor. Jamie on the end of the telephone if she needed him — even Kenneth Gray in an emergency. Pull yourself together, woman.

She should do the job for which she'd been trained through all those long exhausting years. She needed to stop remembering that this was her father in the bed, who might — or might not — be going to die. She wasn't going to be able to cure him miraculously by any sort of agonised yearning over his bed; what she had to do was to look after him with all the skill she possessed. She had to stop being blinded by her love, take two steps back, assess him as if he were any sixty-year-old with a heart problem.

She crossed the room to the bed, and went over him meticulously, as though the professor of medicine himself were at her shoulder. She had to get to know his body and its every infinitesimal change as well as a nurse specialling him would, yet with the additional clinical knowledge and experience she had acquired as a highly qualified physician. From Mortimer's. This was the sort of communion she needed to have with him, not the selfish, demanding love of an over-anxious child.

She succeeded in switching her thoughts successfully into rigorous consideration of varying lines of possible treatment, and was frowning over calculations involving dosages, potassium levels, and her longed-for laboratory investigations, when one of the night auxiliaries came in with a mug of tea. 'Sister thought you might be ready for this.'

The drink was welcome, but she seemed barely to have finished it when Abby herself came in.

'How's the patient?'

'All right so far,' Gina said cautiously, surreptitiously crossing her fingers.

'I just wanted to tell you, there'll be some supper in about half an hour.'

'Supper?' As she spoke Gina realised she shouldn't have been in the least surprised. Naturally the nurses had a main meal on duty.

'Yes. We use the microwave in the kitchen,' Abby explained.

This was a side of life in Vicky's that Gina had never come across before, and she was intrigued. 'I didn't actually know there was a microwave, I'm afraid.'

'Oh, yes. We couldn't manage without it, or without our freezer, well stocked with quantities of Menumaster and Lean Cuisine single portions of almost anything you can think of. So if you'd tell me what you'd like, we can put it into the microwave for you when we do our own.'

'Thanks, Abby, that sounds super.' Abby was being kind and thoughtful; she could easily have left her to fend for herself, and so Gina made an effort to whip up a bit of enthusiasm. It was difficult, though, since Daphne's method of dealing with any crisis was always to retire into her kitchen and cook like a maniac, so that on her return home after evening surgery Gina had been greeted by four delicious and choking courses, through which she'd waded conscientiously. 'I did have a fairly big meal earlier,' she thought it reasonable to admit. 'Something rather light, if you have it?'

'A bit of fish, maybe?'

'Great,' Gina said bravely, though her body was sending rebellious messages at the prospect of eating anything whatever before, at the earliest, lunch tomorrow. Why, she wondered, did she find it necessary to please other human beings by eating when they wanted her to?

The answer was easy, of course. It was the result of an upbringing by Daphne.

'I'll see what we have,' Abby was saying. 'Someone will bring it to you here. In about half an hour.'

She departed, and Gina tried to tell herself that a fish dish from the microwave was exactly what she needed at three in the morning. In no time at all it arrived, seafood pasta, on a supper tray holding a tub of yoghurt and honey, too, and a mug of coffee.

Gina sat down in the chair at the end of the bed and got stuck in. In fact, talking to Abby and thinking about the unnecessary meal, and now doing her best to eat it, relaxed her in spite of herself. She sat in the big chair Abby had sent in for her from the rest room, warm and comfortable. Her whirling thoughts ceased to whirl, spaced themselves out, become controllable. Her father was no worse, he was going to come through this critical period—she began to hope. All would yet be well. She'd be able to stop worrying about getting him to St Mark's Intensive Care, and start planning for moving him home to Rose Bank.

She was aroused from this pleasant picture by her head falling forward on to her knees.

She had almost dropped off. Her father might have died while she snored her head off. Shocked, she stood up, walked around the room, checked the monitor, checked her father's pulses.

The door opened. Ross. 'Everything all right?'

She'd never been so thankful to see anyone.

'Yes, he seems to be doing OK so far.'

'Like me to check him over too?'

'Oh, please do,' she said gratefully. Perhaps it was childish of her, but she longed to have her own findings confirmed.

Ross embarked on an academically precise examination of George, while Gina watched them both. Ross's expression was remote, he was wrapped in concentration, his long fingers moved with assured skill and, too, with a gentle surety that fascinated her. Every move he made was as impeccable as his notes had been, she saw. She couldn't fault him.

Did she want to? Certainly not. Not in any way. All she wanted was to be able to trust him utterly, and she knew she could. For ever.

When he'd completed his examination he turned to her. 'Touch wood,' he said, with a slanting smile that lifted her heart, 'I think he's going to come through this first twenty-four hours very nicely.'

'I'm just beginning to dare to hope so myself.'

'Don't hesitate to call me, though, if you need me.'

'It was awfully good of you to arrange to sleep over here,' she said inadequately. She would have liked to have told him it was wonderful of him, and thrown her

arms round him to demonstrate the extent of her
gratitude, but true to her training she repressed this
urge, and gave him no hint of any emotion, her remark
apparently a mere politeness.

'Think nothing of it. I'm often over here in the
course of the night, and it seemed simpler to doss
down in the rest room than to come and go.' This
throwaway remark covered feelings Gina would have
recognised instantly. Ross longed to fold his arms
comfortingly round her and tell her everything was
going to be all right, leave it to him. Tonight she was
not wearing one of her intimidating outfits, but instead
a velvety track suit in a soft lavender. She looked
sweet, exhausted, and vulnerable, and in need of a
cuddle.

Huh. She'd probably bite him if he tried it. Upset
she might be, but not that far gone even if he was—
and considerably to his surprise, at that. Oh, well,
never trust these middle-of-the-night explosions of
tenderness, they seldom led to anything but trouble,
he reminded himself. Get out and leave her to it. Now
is emphatically not the moment for complicating
relationships.

'Why don't you move your chair over there by the
side of the bed?' he suggested, pausing by the door. It
was the only thing he could think of to make the
remainder of her night's vigil even faintly easier. 'Then
as soon as he begins to wake up and take notice, you
can hold his hand and tell him how well he's doing.
There's nothing to be gained by having the chair at the
end of the bed—it just started there because James
wanted me to put my feet up and watch the monitor at
the same time. But you could easily switch everything
round without disturbing the electronics—let me just
shove it across for you before I go.' Without waiting

for a reply, he began heaving the unwieldy old chair round the room.

Gina was touched. It was angelic of Ross to consider her comfort like this. She was enchanted—and then horrified, as she remembered his spinal problem.

'Oh,' she cried, her feelings at last spilling out without control. 'Oh, Ross, it's sweet of you, but do be careful. Oh, let me do it—remember your poor back, my darling.'

They struggled together over the chair, like a pair of determined buyers in a Harrods sale. Ross was furious, too. Did she imagine he was so much of an invalid he couldn't do her a small service like moving a chair?

'There's not the slightest need for you to bother yourself about my back,' he snapped, and his black eyes met hers without any affection whatever.

In fact, Gina thought, he was looking at her as if he hated her. She bit her lip, stepped back, and tried not to collapse into childish tears in front of him. She'd said the wrong thing again.

Ross finished steering the chair to its new position. 'Try that,' he remarked curtly. 'And don't hesitate to call me if you need any assistance.' He trod a little heavily across the room—he had indeed put too much strain on his back—and let himself out with hauteur, his expression bleak and forbidding.

CHAPTER EIGHT

At eight o'clock in the morning, Amrit appeared. 'How is he?' she asked.

'Fine,' George himself told her cheerfully. 'Absolutely fine. I seem to have had a minor coronary episode, from which I've luckily made a complete recovery. Pay no attention to this daughter of mine if she tries to tell you anything else—she's just an alarmist.' He was sitting up in bed, propped against a mound of pillows, a good colour, with a cup of tea on his bedside table.

'As you see,' Gina said, 'he's OK, and a bit obstreperous.' She gave an exhausted but very genuine smile.

'Send Gina off home, Amrit. She ignores what I say, but perhaps she'll listen to you. She should never have been here all night—a clear case of over-anxiety.'

'I'm going to stay with you now, in any case,' Amrit said. 'Gina, James said you were to go straight home and have breakfast, then be back in surgery for nine o'clock as usual. After that he'll see George himself and we can plan the next stage between us.'

'Look,' George insisted, 'there isn't any next stage. I had a particularly nasty attack of angina, that's all and now I'm over it. Finish.'

Amrit gave him her gentle smile. 'Which I am indeed so glad to see,' she agreed. 'The next stage of your recovery, I will say, rather. All right?'

'Have to do for now, I suppose. Until I've seen Jamie.'

116

'Until then you and I will stay here, if you will be so kind as to bear with my company.'

'Amrit, you'd talk the birds out of the trees. It's quite unnecessary, but come along, sit here by me and tell me all the latest. Gina, go home and change and have your breakfast, as Amrit suggests. Go across to the house and reassure your mother, won't you? In fact, it might not be a bad idea if you had breakfast with her, eh?'

'All right, Dad, will do.'

'And James said after morning surgery, and after we've planned George's—er—George's day or two of—of recuperation, shall we say?' Amrit beamed at George, who winked at her. 'Good. We shall. After that, James says, you are to go home again and go to bed until evening surgery. All right?'

'All right,' Gina agreed, but her response was plainly unwilling.

Amrit made shooing motions with her hands. 'Off you go, then.'

'All right, I've gone,' Gina said, blew her father a kiss from the door, and departed. She collected the Jaguar from outside the surgery on the other side of the road, and drove to Rose Bank.

True to form, her mother set before her one of her most superb breakfasts. Freshly squeezed grapefruit juice, grilled bacon, scrambled egg, sausage, and grilled tomoato, with wholemeal toast and her own marmalade, and a big pot of hot strong coffee. Luckily Gina found she was actually hungry again, and demolished the meal while giving Daphne an optimistic account of George's night and his present condition.

'When can I go in and see him?' Daphne wanted to know. 'Shall I go in with you at surgery time, and sit with him until you're free again? Then you could bring me back here again before you have your sleep.'

'Ross was intending to sit with him this morning,' Gina said slowly, not sure what line to take.

'Oh, well, then perhaps I'd better not interrupt them,' Daphne said at once. 'He'll be all right with Ross,' she added confidently.

Gina was amazed to find that she entirely agreed with this snap judgement of her mother's. George would indeed be all right with Ross. She herself could go to bed and safely sleep all day. Meanwhile the sun was pouring into the gleaming kitchen where they sat, lighting up the pottery, sparking off the glass cafetière and the tiled worktop, silvering Daphne's curls. Home again, another day, and nothing was as bad as she had imagined yesterday.

She pushed her chair back. 'Must hurry. I have to shower and change, and I've less than twenty minutes before surgery. I'll talk to Dad and Jamie, and fix a time for you to go in, soonest. In the meantime, honestly, Ma, he is much, much better. So not to worry more than you can help.' She kissed her and fled across to her own flat over the garage.

Nearly two hours later, surgery over, she went into James's room with her coffee. Amrit followed her, but James at once asked her to go over to Vicky's and relieve Ross.

'He was the first of us to deal with George,' he said. 'So I think we must have him here while we think about the next stage. By now he probably knows more about George's condition than any of us. So if you wouldn't mind, Amrit?'

'Of course not. I'll stay with him until one of you comes over.'

She departed, and Gina sat down in the patient's chair opposite James's desk. He assumed a cheerfulness he wasn't wholly experiencing in order to boost Gina's morale. 'Well, he's weathered the first critical twenty-four hours successfully—more than we dared hope yesterday.' At the moment, Gina looked a good deal worse than George, in fact. Exhausted and dejected, worn out—and no wonder. 'Once we've settled the next move, Gina, you go straight off home and get your head down. Don't attempt to surface until evening surgery. You can leave your list with me, I'll see it gets taken care of.'

Ross came in and sat in the spare chair. 'Hi,' he said. 'Patient continuing his improvement, and raring to go.'

'Somehow we have to persuade him to take it slowly,' James said. 'Lord knows how. However, at least we don't need to have one of us actually on the spot with him in Vicky's any longer, though I think we have to have someone on immediate call right through the weekend. For today, I suggest that should be you, Ross, as it will fit in with your usual commitments. What's more, you'll be in and out of Vicky's in any case, so you can drop in on George without it being obvious to him we're monitoring him. All right?'

'Fine,' Ross said.

'Gina?'

'Yes, fine, of course. And Kenneth Gray will be here this evening, so that's really as far as we need to look for now, wouldn't you say? At some stage Dad's going to need investigation in St Mark's, of course, but——'

'One thing at a time, my dear. We can talk about that sort of thing with Kenneth this evening. This is as far as we need to go now. You go home and get some sleep—we want you on form this evening. I've asked Kenneth to come back for a meal at my place after he's seen your father, so that we can have a comfortable discussion about him, and I hope you'll join us then?'

'Thank you very much, Jamie, I'd like that—oh, and before I go, I promised Mother I'd fix a time for her to go in and see Dad.'

'Leave it with me. I'll have a word with him, and give her a ring. Now off you go.'

'See you this evening, then.'

As the door shut behind her, James sighed, and his eyes met Ross's. 'She's exhausted, poor lass,' he said. 'And frightened out of her wits in a way I've never seen her before. She and George have always been very close. I'm afraid I should have been firmer last night, not given in and allowed her to take over like that.'

Ross shook his head. 'She's paid a price, of course. But I think you were almost certainly right to let her have her way—she was far too stressed to have had much sleep last night, I'd guess. Now, though, she's tired out, and the outlook for George is that much better, so the chances are she'll drop straight off and get six hours' sound sleep. That's my opinion, Doctor.' He gave James a slanting smile.

James found it an undeniable comfort. 'Maybe you're right. I hope so. Now, as far as George is concerned, it seems to me the next problem we're going to have to deal with is how soon to let George go home. If we listened to him he'd be back in time for lunch, whereas my guess is Gina's going to want him kept in Vicky's—if not St Mark's—for weeks on end. We can see what Kenneth says this evening, but what are your feelings about it?'

'On the whole, I'd be in favour of letting him go home, provided he continues to improve.'

'I agree. He's weathered this episode — touch wood — and what he wants is peace and quiet in his own familiar surroundings, if you ask me. Of course, he may have another coronary, we have to be prepared for that, but I'm blowed if I'm going to plan for nothing else. I've always been a believer in keeping heart patients quietly at home whenever reasonably possible. Most of them do better there. What we have to ensure is that somehow George stays right off work and away from all demands from the practice — even reports from any of us on his pet patients. He has to be right out of touch. No telephone calls, for instance. As I see it, if we let him go home, it'll have to be on the strict understanding that he doesn't go near a telephone. And he mustn't set foot in this place for weeks, if not months.'

'I'm with you all the way.'

'We must see what Kenneth has to say tonight, but I'd be surprised if he disagrees.'

'Good. Now, as far as handling George's work is concerned, very shortly I'll be able to take on more — my Volvo's ready for me, and with it I can start doing his home visits as we agreed. I was going to collect it on Monday, but —'

'Go ahead and collect it, then.'

'But —'

'Provided George stays in the clear for the next couple of days, that is. But if he continues to improve, Gina and Amrit and I should be able to stagger through Monday's work. It's your day off anyway — and you've earned it, I will say — so you go and fetch your car, and then from Tuesday on you can think about doing house calls. That will certainly make a difference to running the practice without George, though I think, to start with, you'd better play safe and not take on first visits, when what may be ahead of you is unknown. Just do follow-ups at first.'

'That seems a bit feeble. I could manage to cope with new cases, it seems to me,' Ross protested.

'Feel your way to begin with, like a sensible chap. That's the advice you'd give anyone else, you know that.'

Ross smiled ruefully. 'True. OK, I'll play it your way.'

'Good. Well, I think that's about as far as we can go at present, so George is in your hands until this evening when Kenneth sees him—oh, and don't forget, you're coming to dinner with us afterwards.'

'Are you sure it won't be a bit much? You'll have Kenneth Gray and Gina. I could easily——'

'I may need your support, so don't back out.' James grinned lopsidedly.

'Right. I'll be there.'

These plans, however, came to nothing. Daphne had been out of the action for too long, and she seized the one method that never failed her of regaining the initiative. Everyone was invited to Rose Bank for dinner, she insisted.

As his wife Meg told James over a hurried lunch of rolls, cheese and coffee at their kitchen table, Daphne had a point. 'She says while you're all working flat out for George, she's done nothing, and you must at least allow her to cook for you tonight.'

James sighed. 'It's a bit of a complication, though. We were planning to discuss George's treatment no holds barred. We can't do that if Daphne's there at the head of the table.'

'It's all right. I've fixed that bit.' Before their marriage, Meg had been an outstanding ward sister at St Mark's, renowned for her skill as an unobtrusive fixer, a forestaller of potential troublemakers. 'I explained that you'd be bound to want to have a clinical discussion, and her presence would inhibit this. So she said she'd leave a buffet meal ready, Gina can be hostess, and she'll join George in Vicky's.'

'Brilliant, love. Thanks.'

'Actually she jumped at it,' Meg assured him. 'I think she did just genuinely want to be useful, and that was all. She seemed delighted to hand over to Gina, too—I must say, Gina is being tremendously good with poor old Daph. She's moved back into her bedroom in Rose Bank to be near her, and she's told her she'll stay on after George goes home, to be on the spot. Considering how much she's always valued her independence, and how she loathes being fussed over by Daph, she's really come up trumps.'

'She's a loyal daughter to both her parents, isn't she? Poor lass, she's finding it hard going at present. I can't see any way we can ease it for her, though I'd like to.'

Meg shook her head. 'The need is there, she's meeting it, and no one else can.'

Kenneth Gray arrived quite early that evening, examined George with James, Gina and Ross in dutiful attendance as his entourage, and Abby too—quite like real hospital medicine, as James muttered *sotto voce* to Ross—and finally had an encouraging word with Daphne. 'He's doing very nicely. Much improved since I saw him yesterday—thanks to the excellent care he's been receiving. You really need not have too much anxiety about him—we can justifiably hope he'll go on

improving, and that what he experienced was little
more than what we can look on as a useful warning.'
Daphne's eyes were glued to his, and her body was
tense with controlled anxiety, he could see this—in
fact all of them could. 'Do try not to worry too much,'
he added, patting her tiny shoulders, and taking both
her hands into his. 'So now the four of us are going to
talk over our findings, and plan the optimum management between us. Afterwards this clever daughter of
yours will explain it to you, and you'll know better
how to proceed to take care of him. In the meantime,
I'm told you've very nobly provided not only a venue
for our discussion, but an evening meal for us all. So
very kind and thoughtful, especially when you've had
such a lot on your mind. Much appreciated, I do assure
you.' He relinquished her hands and patted her again.

Daphne was totally won over. She smiled radiantly,
and thanked him profusely for all he was doing for
George. 'I have absolute confidence he's going to be
all right under your care,' she assured him.

James, Gina and Ross, all three of whom had been
afraid Kenneth was a bit over the top, heaved sighs of
relief. They set off in a procession of three cars, led by
Gina in the Jaguar, to Rose Bank.

Here salmon mousse with cucumber and mint in
yoghurt awaited them at the table, chicken breasts in
a mushroom sauce simmered in the slow cooker
plugged in on the sideboard, potatoes in their jackets
were to be found in the hot cupboard. There were
bowls of green salad, and George's best Chablis on
ice. After this came one of Daphne's famous trifles,
followed by coffee from the machine on the sideboard,
with home-made petits fours and truffles.

'That fantastic spread undoubtedly oiled the wheels,
wouldn't you say?' James asked Ross afterwards.

'I'm sure — and what a spread it was.' Ross whistled. James was dropping him off at the flat over the surgery on his own way home.

'Kenneth shed his exhaustion,' James was continuing. 'Fresh as a daisy again, on top of his form. I did think he was a bit heavy-handed with Daph earlier —'

'Me, too.'

'But it worked — he's not Halchester's leading cardiologist for nothing. And as for Gina — she was as putty in his hands, wasn't she? No more problems over George's management in the immediate future, praise be. I think it's because Kenneth talks hospital-speak and Gina feels secure with it, knows where she is. I tend to be an expert in colloquial-speak, and I don't think Gina trusts it.'

Ross was taken by surprise at his reaction to this comment. Far from despising Gina for being so pedantically taken in by mere cardiological word-spinning, his heart was torn by her inability to accept without pain and overwhelming doubt any treatment proposed for her father. 'She's having a perfectly horrible time,' he reminded James. What could he be doing, speaking for her? He couldn't imagine, but he was unable to stop. 'It's natural she should turn to the hospital pundit when it's her father's life that's at stake. Anyway, it seems to have worked out the way we hoped it would, doesn't it?'

'Couldn't be better,' James agreed. He drove into Vicky's drive. 'I'll just go in and explain it all to George and Daph,' he said. 'Then perhaps they'll both have a good night's sleep.'

'I'll come in with you. I still have my late round to do, and in any case I think I may as well sleep here in

Vicky's tonight again, just to be on the safe side. More in the nature of touching wood than from necessity.'

'Are you sure that's all right? If anyone is, you're due a good night's sleep in your own bed.'

'No problem. I can sleep more or less anywhere.'

'It would certainly add to my own peace of mind.'

'No reason why I shouldn't sleep here tomorrow night too. And then——'

'Someone else can take over tomorrow night, if we still feel it's advisable. You've done enough.'

'Ah, but I have an ulterior motive. If George is going home to Rose Bank on Sunday as we're planning, I thought I might take off for London the same day to collect the Volvo on Monday.'

'Right. I agree to that. You can see George off from Vicky's on Sunday morning when Gina collects him, and after that you're off duty until Tuesday. Once Gina drives that Jag of hers out of here with George inside, you're off.'

However, Daphne succeeded in disrupting these plans, too. 'Oh, no,' she said. 'No, Ross, we can't abandon you like that, after all you've done. And are doing. And on Sunday, too.' The green eyes so like Gina's stared meltingly into his. 'You must come back to Rose Bank with George, and have a proper Sunday lunch before you leave for London.'

Since this invitation was enthusiastically seconded by George, Ross felt he could hardly refuse. Nor was he entirely sure he wanted to, even if it did mean a later getaway than he'd planned.

CHAPTER NINE

SUNDAY lunch at Rose Bank, of course, turned out to be another of Daphne's feasts. Ice-cold scoops of melon mingled with shiny black grapes, followed by roast turkey with cranberry sauce, the crispest of roast potatoes and sprouts with chestnuts. In addition, in the middle of the table, a great wooden bowl of lettuce, watercress, cucumber and tomato. This, Daphne informed them, was for George, but if anyone liked to help themselves, there was plenty.

'Plenty of everything, as always, my dear,' George said, a trifle wistfully, 'I only wish I could eat it all, too, but Gina and Ross both have their eyes on me, so I'll restrict myself to a few slices of turkey without any stuffing and some salad. I won't even touch the roast potatoes.' He sighed, and his eyes were longing, they all saw. 'No, I've learnt my lesson, and I'm definitely going to reduce by two stone in the next two months. There, all three of you heard me, and you can keep me to it. A glass of wine, Ross? A rather nice dryish Chablis, I think you'll find.'

'An extremely nice Chablis, and a fantastic meal to go with it,' Ross said. It was no more than the truth. 'It seems wicked to accompany it by talk of a strict diet to slim you down, but I think we should, you know.'

'I entirely agree,' Gina backed him at once. 'I've been explaining to Ma, haven't I? About how vital it is to slim Dad down, and as soon as possible.'

'Yes, dear, you have,' Daphne agreed, with noticeable absence of enthusiasm.

Paying no attention to this, Gina weighed in with what amounted to a teaching hospital lecture on diet in heart disease.

She must have looked like this on a ward round at Mortimer's, Ross thought, and he wished he'd been with her on some of them. Her angular face was all intelligence, her wide mouth fascinatingly mobile, while the green eyes shone vividly with intellectual fervour. She was stimulating company, and he enjoyed her in this mood. But then it was becoming clearer to him by the hour that he enjoyed her in every mood. She was his fate, though whether for joy or desolation he had no idea. Either way, the outlook unnerved him as much as it attracted him. But he drank her in avidly, as she sat opposite him at the round table in the window, wearing another of her velour jumpsuits, this one in soft terracotta, a silky striped scarf knotted at her throat. She looked, he thought, wonderful.

Daphne stood up well to the instructions spinning across the table at her at first, but eventually she began to look harassed, and finally clattered out to the kitchen to fetch the next course with an unmistakable air of escape, refusing, as usual, to allow any of them to join her.

'No, not even you, Gina. Stay exactly where you are. I prefer to manage on my own, thank you.' The tone was tart.

She returned with gooseberry flan and cream. 'The first of this season's gooseberries,' she announced. 'I picked them myself after breakfast. The pastry is made with butter, I'm afraid.' It was a challenge rather than an apology. 'However, there's gooseberry fool made with yoghurt for you, George, so don't suggest, anyone, that I haven't been profiting from my daughter's instructions.' The green eyes stabbed across the table.

'I know it's maddening, Ma.' Gina was as amiable as if she'd been dealing with an unreceptive patient in the clinic. 'But we're all agreed we need to slim Dad down, aren't we?'

'And with as little delay as possible,' Ross added. 'Though I do see that slimming in this household demands a degree of fortitude I know I'd find incredibly difficult.'

Daphne was stung. 'I'm not trying to make things difficult for you, George. You don't think that, do you?'

'It's just that you are such a truly splendid cook, my dear. It is hard to resist your meals, exactly as Ross says.'

Daphne stared at him. 'You mean yes,' she said baldly. 'What you mean is, yes, I am making things difficult.'

George looked worried. Gina tensed and her back stiffened. Ross wondered if George would have another coronary on the spot, and grasped for the first time that there might have been better judgement than he had realised behind Gina's anxiety to have her father removed to St Mark's, twenty miles away.

'Any cook as outstanding as you are is going to have no problem at all in learning a new language of culinary expertise.' Ross took a chance and addressed Daphne directly. 'Someone like you will have no problem, either, in understanding low-fat cooking and menu-planning. You'll easily be able to invent menus that aren't in the least boring for George.' Was he overdoing the flannel? Better go on. Keep trying. 'He's immensely lucky to have you to slim him down with cordon-bleu expertise.'

Hook, line and sinker. Daphne púrred. 'I'm sure I'll be able to see to it, Ross. You must tell me what books to read, and I'll go straight into town tomorrow and get them.' The green eyes, so like Gina's, glowed warmly now, and Ross, briefly diverted, wondered if her daughter's eyes would ever glow like that for him alone? Hastily he pulled himself together. Should he now offer Daphne a reading list, or should he remind her that Gina could supply it? She'd hardly go for that. On the other hand. . .

George, who had relaxed when Ross took Daphne over, put his oar in. 'You'll have a reading list as long as your arm before you can turn round, my dear,' he told her. 'Ross will give you one, so will I, and so will Gina—and James too, no doubt, as soon as you mention it, and Amrit will give you recipes for all those nutritious vegetarian dishes she produces.'

'A whole new culinary experience,' Daphne commented. 'You know,' she said bravely, 'I'm really rather looking forward to it, I think. I'll widen my horizons.'

'You were brill, Ross,' Gina told him as she drove him to Northborough station for the only fast London train of the afternoon. 'If you hadn't been there to handle Ma, I don't know what would have happened. I'm bad with her, I'm afraid. I get impatient, and exasperated, too easily. But you managed her in exactly the right way—she'll be terrific now. She's on her mettle, and she's practically going to make a new career out of cooking for slimmers. Dad won't know what's hit him.'

'It was a dicey moment, I must say. I thought your father might have another coronary on the spot—that was why I went into action fast, and laid it on so thick.

I was afraid I might be overdoing it, but it seemed to work.'

'I'll say it worked.' For a flick of a second, she took her eyes off the road ahead, and gave him that glowing green look he loved. 'You were inspired.'

'It made me realise, though, why you'd originally wanted to get him safely away and into St Mark's.'

She shook her head decisively. 'That wasn't my only reason,' she told him. 'Not even the main one. Some of it was instinctive, I think. I wanted him out of my hands, into hospital, and investigated up to the hilt. A childish panic reaction, no more. Kenneth said I was mistaken, that he'd be better at home, and the investigations could wait, and I accept his opinion. Anyway, it's perfectly true, as James says, that Dad's used to Ma, he can take her in his stride. And when he can't, she causes him far less stress than he'd experience in dealing with starchy young sisters and enthusiastic newly qualified housemen, where he'd be suspicious all the time that they'd bungle something or the machinery would let him down at the crucial moment.'

'Yes, that's the snag about being a doctor admitted to hospital. No faith in the system. You know too much, you distrust the juniors, and you keep your eyes peeled because you are convinced something's going to go wrong.'

'Yes, you're right. He'd be on edge the entire time. I'm sure now that Kenneth was right in thinking he should stay quietly at home. The trouble was I got carried away by an infantile longing to tuck him safely up in bed in the great big hospital.' She chuckled, an endearing sound that made Ross want to hug her. 'In my childhood, hospitals were miraculous places, where people went to bed, were ministered to by gods and goddesses in white coats or starched dresses with caps and aprons — in those days, when we played doctors and nurses, I was always the nurse, in a big white cap, stroking the fevered brow and handing instruments to the doctor.' The green eyes were dancing. ' Later on, I used to imagine myself helping Dad as the practice nurse, and then, as soon as I was old enough, I started to help out at Vicky's in the holidays. To begin with — I was only fourteen or fifteen — it was just taking round the tea or the hot drinks, or occasionally reading the paper to elderly patients. Sometimes I'd help with the library trolley, too. But as soon as I was sixteen I worked there regularly as an auxiliary out of term time, and I can't tell you how important I felt. I was quite puffed up with pride and a sense of achieve-ment — really quite as much as when I finally qualified in medicine. My dream then was simple. To end up as sister-in-charge at Vicky's.'

'So why didn't you?'

'Oh, that particular dream faded. It seemed to last for ages, as teenage dreams tend to, but I suppose in fact it didn't survive more than two holidays. I began to see beyond Vicky's, to St Mark's, and I worked on the wards there for the second year, until I left school. And by then my dream was different again — I was there standing by the bed in a white coat, people handing things to *me*.' She laughed reminiscently, and suddenly, amazingly, the anxiety about her father dissipated, and happiness flooded her. Telling Ross about her childhood dreams and ambitions was for some extraordinary reason immensely satisfying.

'So you went to Mortimer's.'

'And I loved it. The challenge, the stimulus — the road ahead seemed brilliant. But then I changed again, and it all went sour on me.'

He was jolted. This was the opposite of anything he'd expected. 'Not *Mortimer's*?'

She nodded. It was a relief to unburden herself, and come out with the truth. 'Mortimer's. High-powered hospital medicine. The professorial medical unit. Everything that had been my greatest ambition, the stuff of my dreams. I couldn't make it out. There I was, doing what I'd always longed to do, and somehow it wasn't working. Life was a drag. I was at odds with myself. I'd strained every nerve to get there, but then I discovered I didn't like it.'

'It's a very hard grind — are you sure you weren't simply overtired, and because of that depressed temporarily?'

She laughed shortly. 'That's what I tried to tell myself.'

'It does happen,' he said gently.

'It does. But it didn't wear off, and there was more wrong than that. I hated the person I was turning into. I'd gone into medicine, as I said, filled with a real belief in caring, the healing touch, all that — and where had it gone? I was tired, and rushed, and the people I'd once longed to help had turned into tricky problems that I needed somehow to solve and dispose of so that I could move on to the next problem on the list. Caring and compassion had got lost on the way to the top.'

Once again, he wanted only to hold her close and tell her everything was going to be all right from now on, just leave it to him. Almost certainly he would never have said it anyway, but there was no chance even to begin. They were turning into the station forecourt, drawing up in the first space available.

'Here we are,' she said. 'And you've precisely three minutes to catch the train, and I'm afraid you have to cross over the bridge to the other platform. See you.'

He wanted to stay and talk for the rest of the afternoon. Instead he thanked her briskly for the lift, and set off across the pavement without a backward glance.

She sat and watched him go. If only he'd been able to stay. All she wanted to do was to go on sitting in the Jag outside the station for ever, talking to him.

She wouldn't see him again until Tuesday or Wednesday. It seemed an age. And then they'd very likely pass at speed in the corridor, no chance for a brief word, let alone to confide her childhood dreams, the collapse of her ambitions. She reversed the Jag and drove miserably home, the happiness that had spun across her day vanished, leaving no trace.

Tuesday at last came, and, after morning surgery, Amrit — who had taken over Gina's midder case — departed in a hurry to meet the social worker at the caravan, from which the new mother refused to budge. Gina and James were left, dividing up George's patients between them. As they were doing this, Kenneth Gray's secretary rang to make an appointment for George to spend Wednesday afternoon of the following week at St Mark's for the first of the planned investigations.

'I would quite like to go over with him, if you think I could be spared,' Gina said. Her father had impressed on her that James, in his own absence, was the senior partner.

'Wednesday's your day off in any case, so it's your own free time you'll be giving up,' he pointed out kindly.

'Well, yes, in theory, but I wasn't actually proposing to take it, not the way we are.'

'I don't believe in going without days off,' James

said firmly. 'A bad habit, and counter-productive. If your father had taken proper hours off as well as on, we wouldn't be where we are today, that's my opinion. Ross will have his car from now on and he'll be doing house calls, so I reckon we should be able to stagger along without you one day a week — have your full day off tomorrow and next week. This week you certainly need it. You've been on all weekend, after all.'

'I could easily——'

'Let's plan for you to have Wednesday as usual, this week and next, but if anything does crop up, we'll call you in. All right?'

'Fine. Thanks, Jamie.'

Ross was driving his new Volvo down the motorway, his spirits higher than they'd been for years. He was back at the wheel of his own car, and going places, too. And when he reached Northborough, not only a job awaited him — and one he was beginning to enjoy — but also that entrancing Gina.

He was going to date her, and dine her and wine her, and finally — but not that finally, quite soon, with any luck — he was going to make wild passionate love to her. The two of them would set the world on fire with their loving.

Life was on the move. The long painful years of his accident, its treatment, and then his rehabilitation were behind him. Opportunities were opening up, too. Leo had told him there was another post in the offing he could have if he liked to go after it, so he didn't even any longer have to make a choice between either general practice or a management post. The director of research at International Pharmaceuticals was retiring in the autumn, apparently, and he'd been asking around at his old teaching hospital in search of a successor. They wanted a clinician, to deal with the doctors participating in the big drug trials, so Ross, with a stint in general practice behind him in addition to his hospital experience, would be in an excellent position to apply, Leo said.

He had to think seriously about it. It was a tremendous opportunity — most of his friends would say he needed his head examining if he turned it down in favour of the long hours and stresses of general practice. But he was enjoying the Northborough practice in a way he hadn't enjoyed work since his injury had removed him so abruptly from the operating theatres.

He owed something to George, too. George had been willing to take him on, as an unknown quantity, and now the boot was on the other foot. George was going to have to slow up, and almost certainly he'd find this easier to accept if he and Ross were able simply to change places — if George now became the part-timer and Ross the full-timer — than if the practice had to find someone entirely new. However, at the same time George would never want him to pass up this chance merely on the grounds that it would be convenient for the practice.

He'd have to wait and see. He had a month in hand, before he need put in for the drug post. He could talk to James about it, see what he thought.

And meanwhile there was Gina. He was going all out to get her. That was definite. And what was more, exciting as the prospect of making love to her was, that was by no means the whole story. He was serious about Gina, that had been becoming clearer to him with every day that passed. She was his fate. He was on the way to a partnership for life.

What if she didn't think so? After all, what did he have to offer her? An ex-surgeon with a damaged body and a problematic future, either in general practice or with a drug firm. He wasn't much of a catch these days.

To hell with that. Gina, here I come.

Turn me down if you can.

When Gina arrived back, a little late for evening surgery, there was a long white Volvo estate parked next to James's Renault. Who was that? Could it be. . .? It was.

'Ross's new car,' Betty told her at once. 'He arrived back at teatime. He's doing evening surgery.'

Her heart lifted, but all she said was, 'I'm afraid I'm a bit late. You'd better send the first one in straight away.'

The evening, though, was to prove difficult. She had several awkward patients with complicated histories or insoluble and ongoing problems, all of whom needed a good deal of time, and then she had to take even longer over a new patient with Parkinsonism who'd just moved into Northborough—and whose records, needless to say, had failed to arrive. When she finally sent him on his way, Betty told her that, as she'd been running late, Ross had cleared most of her remaining patients, except for one who had elected to wait for her—however long it took. When she heard who it was, her heart sank. Heather Broomfield had come for her usual weekly dose of moral support.

Gina apologised for keeping her so long.

'Not your fault, Doctor. And I did want to see you particular, so I thought I wouldn't see the other doctor. I've been so worried, you see, and I didn't think he'd understand about Daise. But you know all about her, and you can tell me what you think.'

Reluctantly Gina sat back to listen to another instalment of the long-running saga that was Heather Broomfield's family life. She had three daughters living at home and usually in the midst of feverish and unsuitable affairs, or so their mother felt, and Gina knew that being able to unburden herself of her anxieties in the surgery was a lifeline for her, and she'd never so far succeeded in finding a method of cutting her short. Heather had problems enough without her daughters, in any case—she was overweight and breathless, had constant trouble with her gall bladder, tended to comfort-eating of the wrong foods for her condition, mainly because of her anxieties about her daughters, and suffered from bronchitis every winter.

Eventually she left, with profuse thanks and the prescription she needed in her hand. 'I feel so much better, Doctor, now I've told you all about it. Thank you ever so much. I'm afraid I've kept you.'

'No, of course not,' Gina assured her. 'It's what I'm here for.'

The door shut behind her. Gina ran her hands through her hair, pulled a face—more at herself than at poor Heather—and began writing up her records. After that, she thought, her spirits rising, she'd look in on Ross and have a word with him about his Volvo.

But when she came out into the hall, the surgery was silent and deserted, all doors wide. Everyone had gone. The Volvo was there, so presumably Ross was upstairs in his flat, but she could hardly burst in on him, interrupt his evening meal, demanding he tell her all about his new car.

She shrugged resignedly. Daphne would have her own meal waiting, and she hadn't seen her father since lunch, more than six hours ago. Time she checked on him. But tomorrow would be her day off, and James had been adamant she was to take it. She wouldn't see

Ross until Thursday now. She banged the big front door behind her, unlocked the Jaguar, and set off for Rose Bank.

Only a few minutes later Ross, who'd been over to Vicky's to look at a new admission with the patient's own doctor, came back, saw the Jaguar had gone, and experienced the same sag of the spirits as Gina. He'd been planning to ask her for a drink, or even a meal, if she happened to be free. He'd have to leave it until tomorrow. He'd ask her at coffeetime, fix something then, and book a table — at Chez Guillaume, say.

However, he was out of luck. The next morning at coffee, of course, James told him Gina was having her day off. 'I made her take it. She's worn out. Do her good.'

'Yes, of course. I'm sure you're right,' Ross said at once. What was twenty-four hours, anyway? Nothing.

It didn't feel like nothing. It felt like Black Wednesday. He had to pull himself together. And he could take this chance when they were on their own together to put James in the picture about the offer from the drug firm, and sound him out on how to proceed. Useful, really.

James's long face lengthened at the news. 'In the autumn?' he repeated. 'I'd been hoping you'd be able to stay here with us a good deal longer than that, I must say. We all had. Still, it's a splendid opportunity, I suppose.' He looked mournful.

Ross was relieved to see it — that was one of his queries answered. They did want him to stay on. 'Trouble is,' he said, 'I don't really want it.'

'Why not?' James asked, though his face lit up.

'Because I'd rather stay here, as long as I'm going to be fit enough. That's what I wanted to talk to you about, if you can spare a few minutes.'

'Of course. Glad to.'

'About house calls.'

'We agreed you should begin doing them this week, didn't we? Except for new patients.'

'That's my point. I've been wondering how you'd feel about my taking on George's full list straight away. I'd soon find out then if I can cope with the workload — and we'll all know how much use I'm going to be to you. So what do you think?'

'What are you proposing to do if you have one of your bouts of postural hypotension while you're with a patient, or between patients?'

'Sit tight and wait for it to pass. Or ring for assistance, if the patient should be some sort of emergency. I've got a car phone.'

'Ah, you have. Excellent. That does make a difference. Right. As far as I'm concerned, you take on George's list and see how you go. But on one condition only. You're to come clean and ask for help if you have the slightest doubt at any point. No keeping it to yourself. I want regular reports from you, so that we can monitor your progress together.'

'I'll keep you in touch, I swear.'

'Good. Now, let's suppose all goes well, and we find you can handle it, would you think of staying here with us in Northborough permanently?'

'Nothing I'd like better, provided I'm sure I can pull my weight.'

'Great. I'm delighted to hear it. We'd certainly like to have you. So when do you have to decide about this drug firm?'

'I've got a month.'

James shook his head. 'Not really long enough for a proper assessment.'

'But long enough to provide a clear pointer.

'We'll just have to watch it. We mustn't allow you to take on more than you can handle in the long term, so that you pass up this drug firm offer, but then find you can't stand up to general practice. That wouldn't be at all sensible. However, sufficient unto the day — off you go with George's list and see how you make out.'

Back upstairs in his flat, Ross decided not to hang about. He'd take a chance, ring Chez Guillaume and book a table for the following evening.

Lunatic, really, to suppose that Gina would be free on such short notice. However, he was going to try.

Providence seemed to be on his side, for once. The next day he ran into Gina first thing in the morning, when he was walking back from Vicky's, and she was getting out of the Jag.

'I like your new Volvo,' she told him. 'When we have a moment you must tell me about it.'

Ross's heart turned over, and he spoke sternly to it. Keep pumping, damn you. Now is not the moment to pass out cold at her feet. What he must do was to take her up on her suggestion. 'How about this evening, then? Over a meal at Chez Guillaume, say?'

The green eyes widened, and he was sure she was about to refuse. He'd been a fool to imagine she'd be free at such short notice.

She didn't refuse. She shook her dark hair back, and laughed. 'I must say, you've genned yourself up very effectively on local eating places — Chez Guillaume is the tops. I'd love to. Thanks so much.'

'Eight-thirty, say?' Instead of worrying about passing out, he felt like turning somersaults, as they went up the steps together and into the surgery.

'Fine. I look forward to it.' She gave him her wonderful smile — though admittedly she then bestowed it on Betty as she passed — and went into her room.

Ross also gave Betty a beaming good morning as he went into his own room.

They should both have known better, they agreed afterwards. Perhaps if he hadn't booked, hadn't tempted fate, it would have been different. But it wasn't.

The day was busy from the outset, with a long morning surgery to start with, and an equally long evening one which by no means ended it for either of them. Ross still had two home visits to do after surgery. Gina had two more patients to see, Betty told him as he went through the hall, and at that moment the patient she'd been seeing came out of her room and departed.

'Just let me have a word with her before you send the next one through,' Ross said quickly, and went in himself.

'Sorry,' she apologised immediately he appeared. 'I'm afraid I've still got two more.'

'I know, Betty told me. I've got a couple of visits to fit in, that's what I came to say — so maybe we'll reach the finishing tape together, but I was wondering if it would be a good plan to change the booking to nine o'clock, just to be on the safe side.'

'Last orders nine-thirty, so we'd be OK. Good idea. Tell you what, you clear off and do your visits, and I'll ring Chez Guillame. See you here between eight-thirty and nine, all right?'

'Fine. Thanks very much. On my way.'

All this planning came to nothing, though, as five minutes later Gina had a call from Mrs Winter, saying Susie was coughing badly and fighting for every breath.

'I'll come over. I've one patient to see here, and

then I'll be with you—inside half an hour, say? All right?'

'Thank you, Doctor. I'll be ever so glad to see you— I've never known her quite as bad as this.'

So at a quarter to nine Gina was on her way to Susie. She met Ross en route, returning from his visits, and broke the news to him.

'Rotten luck,' he said. 'We're not going to make it, are we? I'll cancel Chez Guillaume, but maybe we'll be able to snatch a drink and some sort of snack later on at the Rose and Crown—how would that be?'

'Great. I'm awfully sorry, Ross, but I do have to go to Susie.' Gina felt that now she'd finally ruined their precious evening together.

'Of course you do. Not to worry—I'll go over to Vicky's in the meantime and do my round, then the rest of the evening should be clear. I'll see you—either at Vicky's or back here, according to how it works out.'

In fact he was still in Vicky's when Gina rang through from the Winters' house to say she was bringing Susie in *stat*, in her own car, and she'd need the little intensive care ward ready.

Her mother had been right. Susie was worse than she'd ever been.

Ross stayed on at Vicky's to help, and he and Gina and Abby battled for nearly two hours simply to keep Susie alive. Her damaged lungs were at last losing out, her struggling heart was unable to pump enough oxygen round her body to keep her going, and she continued to deteriorate as they worked.

'I think she needs the facilities of St Mark's,' Ross said gently, fearing Gina wasn't going to like giving in and handing Susie over to the hospital in Halchester.

But she surprised him. 'You're right,' she said at

once. 'And sooner rather than later. I'm doing her no favours by trying too long. Can you cope here while I ring St Mark's and the ambulance service?'

'Will do.'

'Luckily we won't have any problem about admission—since she had her appointment there last month they put her on to their open list, so she can go straight in whenever necessary. Oh, I am glad we went ahead and got her that appointment in spite of Dad. Right, back shortly. I hope.'

It took her more time to arrange for the ambulance than to lay on Susie's admission to St Mark's, but she succeeded in rejoining Ross at Susie's bedside within twenty minutes, reporting that the ambulance was on its way. 'How's Susie doing?'

'Fingers crossed, but I'd say no worse. It's possible that our treatment's beginning to work. But it's very dicey still, she could go either way.'

'You're right. I think I'd better go in with her, see her safely installed in St Mark's with my own eyes. I'll just have a word with the Winters and put them in the picture, poor souls—OK if I leave you again to cope here?'

'Go ahead.'

Both the Winters, looking pale and agonised, were sitting in the hall. Gina explained that Susie needed St Mark's, and that the ambulance was already on its way. 'I'll go in the ambulance with her, so if you'd like to follow in the car you can wait there while she's admitted. Or you could go home, and I'll give you a ring and let you know how she's getting on, and you can snatch some sleep and visit her tomorrow.'

The two Winters glanced briefly at one another, and then Mrs Winter said quickly 'I think we'd rather be on the spot, Doctor, thank you all the same. Jason's on his way here, too, so we can take him with us. It usually does Susie good to know he's around, so maybe just to hear he's there ready to join her may help.'

'I'm sure you're right,' Gina agreed warmly. 'A lot depends, and has always depended, on Susie's marvellous fighting spirit. I'll explain to them when we get to St Mark's about letting Jason stay with her, or if they're too busy for that to be practicable, just let her see him for a minute so that she can tell he's around and ready to join her.'

'Aye, he's a good lad, is Jason,' Mr Winter said. 'Susie's been lucky with him, no doubt of that. I wasn't in favour of it to start with, but I reckon it'll be good for Susie to get married.'

And we must keep her alive and see that she does, and that they have years together, Gina thought inwardly, her decision to go with Susie in the ambulance reinforced.

Jason arrived on his bicycle at the same moment as the ambulance drew in. He looked horrified at the sight of it, and Gina, waiting on the steps to brief the crew, flashed him a hasty reassuring smile. 'She'll do better in St Mark's, we decided, Jason — you'll find the Winters inside, in the hall; they'll explain,' before turning back to the ambulance staff.

Susie was transferred to the ambulance, and Gina, before leaving, asked Ross to have a word with Jason to boost his morale a bit.

'Sure. Will do. I'll follow in the Volvo — you're going to need transport back.'

This had already occurred to Gina, but she hadn't been going to mention it, knowing that she could always order a minicab from St Mark's when the time came. 'Are you sure? It may mean quite a bit of hanging around, and I could easily —— '

'No problem. I'll be right behind you.'

'That's truly great. Thanks a million, Ross.' As she climbed into the ambulance behind Susie, the phrase 'I'll be right behind you' was repeating itself in her mind, and although there was not the slightest reason in the world why she herself should be in any need of a boost to her own morale, she realised she knew exactly how Susie felt when Jason was around.

The comforting knowledge stayed with her, and was still there when she and Ross at last left St Mark's together at two in the morning.

'At least she's no worse,' Gina said, as they drove out of the hospital and turned towards the motorway. 'Which at one stage I thought was unlikely. She might just last until morning.'

'Touch wood.'

'Absolutely.' Gina sighed.

'I know what's wrong with you. Low blood sugar. You're depressed. When did you last eat? Twelve hours ago?'

'About that, probably. You too?'

'I had a doughnut oozing home-made jam at the farm with the chicken pox kids around fourish. It was terrific, but it was a long time ago, and I'm sorry to say I haven't the faintest idea where we can drop in at nearly three in the morning and order a gourmet meal.'

'You haven't really had a chance to explore the area yet, have you? Otherwise I'm sure you'd be able to come up with somewhere. But look at me, I'm a real failure. I've lived here all my life—and me dad afore me—but I can't suggest anywhere for so much as sausage and mash.'

'I can,' Ross announced triumphantly. 'The motor-way service station. Coming up.'

'Of course. I should have remembered. I'm ravenous. I honestly don't care what they have, as long as it's food.'

So much for that first date, Ross told himself sourly. Be thankful for small mercies.

They ended up with beans on toast and horrible coffee at a table covered in crumbs and spills, but neither of them cared. The beans tasted of beans and filled the aching void, and by four a.m. Ross drove Gina into the forecourt at the surgery, she thanked him sleepily, got into the Jag, and drove away to Rose Bank.

CHAPTER TEN

As she jogged through the wide gates and up the Rose Bank drive, Gina was met by the scent of lilac drifting on the early morning air. Summer days were on the way. Soon the roses would be out. Already the wistaria—which her father had planted the year she was born—was in bloom above the porch and round the windows, festooning them with a mist of blue.

In the sunny kitchen coffee was filtering, and her mother was preparing breakfast. 'Before you sit down, dear,' she said, 'Kenneth Gray wants you to ring him. He wants to talk about the arrangements for this afternoon. Here's his home number—he said you'd be able to catch him before he leaves.'

'All right. I'll do it from Dad's study. He's upstairs still, isn't he?'

'Yes, he's actually agreed to have breakfast in bed again, so I'll take it up while you're telephoning.'

'Fine. Back shortly.'

Kenneth told her that Sir Joshua Stirling, the eminent cardiologist from the Central London Hospital and his own former chief, was coming down to St Mark's that afternoon to see George with him.

'Oh, good—that's terrific.'

'Isn't it? I was going to sound him out, as a matter of fact, to see if there was any chance he'd be able to fit in a visit to Northborough in the next few weeks, but apparently he'd already heard about George's coronary from Ross Nicholson, so Josh is catching the lunchtime train, and hopes to be with us about three this afternoon. Now, two points. First of all, will you tell your father?'

'Sure. He'll be fearfully chuffed.'

'Secondly, can you get him here by one, instead of two? I want to make sure all our tests are complete when Josh arrives, so we don't have to waste his time.'

'We'll be there by one.'

'Good. Afterwards, I'm giving Josh dinner at Long Barn, and I'd like you to be there with us, so can your mother drive your father home, while you stay on?'

'No reason why not—yes, I'm sure she will, and thank you very much for the dinner invitation. I'll be delighted to join you.'

'That's fixed, then. And James Black ought to be with us, too—after all, he's officially your father's doctor, isn't he? I've already suggested he should come over for a chat after we've done George's tests, so will you bring him up to date? Tell him about Josh, and ask him to be here between five and six, and stay on for dinner at Long Barn.'

'I'm sure he'll be pleased to. Can we leave it that, unless I ring you back, he'll be coming?'

'Fine. Now, there's one more arrangement to fix, if you would. This is for Josh. While he's down in Halchester, he wants to see Ross Nicholson, he says, and he's planning to do it after he's seen your father. So I promised we'd get Ross over to St Mark's by five p.m. Josh wants him to have dinner with us, too. So will you tell him?'

'Oh,' Gina said faintly. 'Yes, I will. Sure.' She was going to see Ross today after all. Well, she'd need to see him if she was to give him Kenneth's message, wouldn't she? And he'd be at the dinner, too.

'Right,' Kenneth was saying cheerfully, pleased to

have unloaded all his chores. 'See you around one, then. In Outpatients.'

'We'll be there,' Gina promised. She put down the telephone and glanced at her watch. Twenty to nine. She'd just be able to catch Ross before surgery, if she left now. Better to see him than telephone, and she could catch James too, and bring him up-to-date on the new arrangements. A small voice informed her waspishly that both these messages could easily be telephoned through, but she ignored it — or, indeed, hardly heard it. It wasn't what she wanted to hear. She rushed through the kitchen, telling her mother that they were now leaving at eleven, not twelve, that she was going over to the surgery, and that she'd explain when she returned.

She drove to the surgery, and parked next to Ross's Volvo. At least he was here, not out on a call. The front door was open — ten to nine, and patients were arriving. Betty was at her desk.

'Ross upstairs still?' Gina asked.

'Er — yes, that's right.' Betty was startled at Gina's abrupt arrival, in her tracksuit, on her day off, and she watched her enter the lift, puzzled, and heard it begin its grinding ascent.

Ross heard it too, and was mildly puzzled, as he stood on the landing ready to go down.

Dark hair and the unnerving green eyes appeared, while his own eyes took in the tracksuit with considerable pleasure. A right armful this morning. He set his jaw and reminded himself he was going for morning surgery.

Gina stepped out of the lift. 'Hi — I have a message for you.'

He took her by the shoulders, holding the heavy doors with his foot, and shoved her back into the lift.

She felt even more delightful than he'd expected, and he thought about stopping the lift between floors and holding her for much longer, though all he said — and crisply, at that — was 'Tell me about it on the way down.'

'Kenneth Gray rang,' she said hastily, unable to understand why she was feeling so disappointed. 'He said Josh Stirling is coming down to see Dad today at St Mark's, and — '

'Oh, great,' Ross said, looking really pleased.

'Something to do with you, I rather gathered?'

'Oh, I started the message on its way, no more than that. But I did hope it might work. And it has.'

They'd reached the hall now, he was holding the lift doors for her, and she had to step past him and continue their conversation in public, which was not how she'd planned. 'There's another part to Kenneth's message,' she told him. 'He said that this afternoon, after he's seen Dad, Josh Stirling wants to see you.' She hated having to deliver this information in the middle of the hall, with patients passing, and Betty drinking in every word they uttered. Ross was always very private about his personal health, and she wished, too late, that she'd been firm when they'd met on the top landing, and not allowed him to hustle her back into the lift so fast. If it hadn't felt so extraordinarily pleasant when he'd done it she would have kept her head and delivered her message at a better moment. She seemed incapable of keeping her head where Ross was concerned. Weird. Or maybe not so weird. She ploughed on. 'After he's seen Dad, Josh Stirling wants to see you. You're to be there by five o'clock, and then afterwards you're invited to stay on for dinner with Josh and Kenneth at somewhere called Long

Barn. I'll be there too, and James, and we're to discuss Dad's condition and management, and so on.'

His face had gone blank. He was divulging nothing. Just as she had feared, he was going to clam up. He was probably furious with her for mentioning all this so publicly.

'Five o'clock at St Mark's,' she said uncertainly.

'I heard you the first time.'

Now he was snapping. She'd handled this hopelessly.

'Thanks,' he added belatedly. 'That's it, then.' He walked past her down the hall towards his room, saying to Betty as he went by her desk, 'First patient, please,' with the same snap in his voice.

So that was that.

Now she had to tell James about the arrangements. She told Betty she needed to slip in and see him between patients, and was able to go in almost immediately, as his first patient was a regular who never needed long.

'Only me,' she said. 'One or two changes about this afternoon — Kenneth's been on.'

'Shoot.'

She told him about Josh, and the dinner party, and then about Ross.

'Good,' James said. 'That all seems excellent. It'll be interesting to know what he thinks about Ross, too. Could hardly have come at a more opportune moment, could it? Josh's opinion is exactly what we all need to help in the decision between International Pharmaceuticals and Northborough.'

'Yes. Yes, you're absolutely right, it is. Oh, I do *hope* he'll be fit enough to stay on here.'

James gave her a speculative look.

Gina knew at once he was asking himself why she

sounded so worked up. Well, why did she? 'Dad'll be so much happier handing over his patients to Ross than to anyone new,' she said hastily. 'And Ma's fallen for him, so anything he says goes—she's really into slimming recipes, because Ross told her last Sunday it was important. I've been saying so for years, and made no impression whatever.' She scanned James hopefully. Had he fallen for what she secretly knew was waffle? She just longed for Ross to stay, period.

All James actually said was that it was very good of Josh to come down especially.

'Fantastic of him. Well, see you later at St Mark's.'

When Ross drove the Volvo into the car park at St Mark's that afternoon, he saw Daphne's Vauxhall, with Daphne herself sitting inside and looking tense. As soon as she saw him, her face lit up, and she scrambled hastily out of the car.

'Oh, Ross, I am glad to see you.'

'Collecting George, are you? Nearly five—he should be just about ready for you. Come along in, and we'll find him.' He held her arm, and steered her towards Outpatients.

'Oh, dear,' she said. 'I do feel so awful. Silly of me, I know, but I simply can't help it. I've been sitting in the car feeling steadily worse and worse. What if——?'

'Now, Daphne, if there's one place where George is in safe hands, it's here, with Josh Stirling, no less, *and* Kenneth Gray to look after him.'

'Oh, I know, I know. I realise I'm being silly—but the trouble is I'm so terrified of what they're going to find, and what they'll say about George.'

'No need to be afraid,' he heard himself say jovially, though he knew exactly how Daphne was feeling. The same as he felt himself. He was dreading being told bluntly after rigorous examination that he certainly must not think of working in general practice, he must guard his precarious health, head straight for International Pharmaceuticals, and think himself lucky to be working at all.

If in fact he wasn't going to be fit for the long hours and uncertain demands of general practice, he had been reminding himself every five minutes as he drove over, obviously he needed to know, and as soon as possible. To dread actually being told was short-sighted and about as silly as you could get. 'I think,' he told Daphne boldly, praying that this would be true for him, too, 'I think you're likely to be given reassuring news this afternoon. Of course George must take care from now on, but my instinct is that if you can keep him right away from the telephone and Vicky's or the surgery for the next six weeks, and if at the same time you can slim him down and see that he starts taking regular exercise, he'll be back at work and none the worse — very likely a good deal better — in three or four months.'

'Oh Ross, thank you. You are cheering me up.'

'Come along in, and let's look for him.'

They found him in a crowded little room at the far end of Outpatients, pale and tired, but perfectly cheerful. He was the one, as it happened, who spotted them as they hesitated in the doorway. 'Hello, you two. Come along in and meet everyone,' he gestured expansively.

Everyone turned out to be the great man himself, Sir Joshua Stirling, KCVO, MD, FRCP, etc etc — he had honorary degrees from almost everywhere anyone had heard of, his reputation worldwide. Physically, though, he was an oddity. No more than five and a half feet in height, but bulky and square, with powerful shoulders, he had a ruddy outdoor complexion — he was a sailing man — piercing blue eyes and a thatch of untidy white hair. He was dressed, as he almost always was, in a hairy tweed capable of standing up alone, and smelling strongly of peat. Patients adored him, and trusted him to the ends of the earth. So did his staff, when they weren't frightened out of their wits or in the middle of one of the rows that erupted daily, if not hourly. Kenneth Gray had once been his registrar.

Crammed into the small room with the great man, beside Kenneth, was Kenneth's registrar, a lanky individual called Tom, his house physician, a physiotherapist, one of the cardiology technicians called Nick, Kenneth's secretary, a ravishing blonde — and, of course, George and Gina, who looked even more exhausted than her father.

'Hah, Ross,' Sir Joshua announced. His voice, easily distinguished across harbours, overrode all else, and eyes swivelled at once.

'Afternoon, sir.'

'Look well,' the bellow asserted. 'However, I'm proposing to run the rule over you, hm?'

Ross muttered almost inaudibly and, as far as Gina could tell, irascibly too, though the great man appeared unmoved, to her relief, and turned back to her father.

'I'll say goodbye, then, George. Go home and look after yourself. Do what we tell you, and you'll likely live to ninety-two. A lean ninety-two, mind. I'll see you in about an hour, Kenneth. All right? Here?'

'I'll be here.'

'Now then, Ross, I want to know, what about this postural hypotension, eh?'

Ross produced some more muttering, but the great

man apparently deciphered it, nodded attentively, while Gina sighed with relief.

'We'll see, anyway,' Sir Joshua added. 'Now, I'm being told you don't want this desk job in International Pharmaceuticals they've found for you. That right?'

'Not if I'm fit enough for——'

'You'd better come along and we'll see about that. We'll wire you up for sound, and have you on the bicycle and then the treadmill. Kenneth, you're lending me Tom, aren't you, and Nick here, too?'

'That's right. Off you go, and I'll see you back here when you're through.'

'Right. Outside, then, my team, and on your way.' Sir Joshua stamped off down the corridor.

Gina hadn't been to Long Barn before. She fell for it at first sight. An old flint building in a fold of the downs, it was a dramatic blend of old and new, with its original oak beams, huge modern windows catching all the light, and, as they entered, a great open staircase climbing to the rafters that supported the roof with its lichened tiles laid centuries earlier. If she hadn't been in a state of idiotic panic about Ross, she would have enjoyed herself hugely. But where was he? Why wasn't he with them? What had happened to him? The most junior member of their little group, she could hardly cross-examine Sir Joshua when he had announced—to Kenneth, in any case, not to her at all—that Ross would follow on later, he'd sent him off with Tom for a bit of a break. 'Tom went over to the residents' quarters with him, and I told him to take it as slowly as he could—we'd rather put Ross through it, y'see.' Josh had laughed comfortably, the noise reverberating through the Outpatient hall, and Gina wanted to kill him. 'I told Tom to follow on when they were both ready, and I'd explain they were going to be a bit late.'

'Fine. Useful, in a way. We're meeting James Black at Long Barn, so we can begin our discussion about George and his future programme, and then when Ross and Tom arrive you'll have time for a talk with him about his problem. And then we'll put you on the London train, Josh, and many, many thanks.'

'Glad to come if needed. Y'know that.' Josh was suddenly gruff.

At Long Barn James was waiting for them, they were quickly ensconced in a bar off the great hall, and plunged into a detailed and highly technical discussion about the exact state of George's heart and arteries, his immediate management, and his chances of a return to a normal working week.

This was her own father they were discussing, Gina told herself furiously. She must lock into every word the great Sir Joshua uttered, not scavenge round in her mind trying to decide what could be happening to Ross. Anyway, she knew perfectly well what was happening. He was being looked after in St Mark's residency by Kenneth's registrar. He could hardly be in better hands.

Hers?

She should be so lucky.

But he'd obviously had a packet, during his hour and a half with Josh. They'd put him through it, and he'd had to be taken away by Tom to recuperate before he was fit to appear at Long Barn for this wretched meal they were all involved in. She was possessed by an urgent, overriding need to join him, to put her arms round him and hold him for ever, safe with her against anything life might throw at him.

Pull yourself together, woman. Ross would soon tell

you where to get off if you tried to do anything so
dotty.

But what had they been doing to him? And why
hadn't she been there to look after him?

Stop this.

Anyway, she knew perfectly well what they'd been
doing to him. She'd just been through it all with her
father. Her heart had not bled then; she'd known the
tests were necessary, and she'd assessed the results
intelligently.

But if Ross had needed to rest afterwards, before he
was fit to face Long Barn and a meal, and had needed
Kenneth's registrar to look after him, what did this say
about his ability to work in general practice? It meant
he couldn't do it, of course. What Ross was going to
be told this evening when — if ever — he arrived, was
that he must take up what was undoubtedly an amazingly good offer from this hideous drug firm.

Goodbye, Ross.

She couldn't bear it. He couldn't be going to walk
away, out of her life forever, just when she'd found
him. She couldn't live without him.

Of course she could. She'd have to. But as she went
in and out of the surgery each day, or looked in on
patients in Vicky's, there'd be no Ross to encounter in
the hall. No Ross to scrap with. No Ross to watch
secretly. That tall angular figure with the head of crisp
dark hair, the beaky and often exhausted features, the
glittering eyes that were almost black, she had decided,
and that possessed the unnerving capacity to look right
through into her soul whenever the mood took him,
but that could, too, melt and caress her heart in a way
no man had ever done before — none of this would she
experience ever again.

They were moving across to the dining-room, saying

they would go ahead without Ross and Tom, because Josh had to catch the London train — oh, darling, darling Ross, what have they been doing to you? — and she went with them, hearing her voice making the appropriate responses, knowing that she'd been participating fully in the discussion, that no one had guessed the turmoil in her mind. Years of training told, she made sensible replies, proffered useful suggestions — even, she could tell, succeeded in making a favourable impression on Kenneth — while, luckily for her, this reliable tape recorder in her head could be counted on to play back to her, whenever she needed them, the questions and answers, even the minor asides, of the discussion.

Another equally competent self seemed to be talking over the menu with Kenneth, and deciding on the smoked trout, followed by the duck braised with black cherries, a speciality, he assured her, of Long Barn's chef.

The smoked trout arrived, a cold wine from the Loire was poured into her glass. At any rate, she thought, she didn't have to drive home at the end of this nightmare, so she could safely take the edge off her agony with this delicious wine, and be thankful for small mercies.

'Drowning your sorrows?' an amused voice behind her enquired.

Ross.

Fighting fit, apparently.

Like an angry mother whose child had escaped disaster, she wanted to shake him. And shout at him.

He walked past her and began apologising to Kenneth for his unpunctuality. He was smoothly confident, incredibly well groomed in expensive suiting, wearing a Central tie and a pristine shirt. That was what he'd been doing, while she'd been tearing herself to shreds. Showering. Changing his shirt.

He sat down opposite her, and began on the smoked trout that someone had evidently ordered for him. His eyes met hers, and she flinched. He was doing it again. Looking straight through into her soul.

Who did he think he was?

Her beloved. Forever.

This certainly was sufficiently arresting for her to have recourse to the Loire wine again, and she found she had drained her glass. Kenneth instantly refilled it, while James began to bring Ross up to date with the decisions about George.

'We are all agreed, I think, that there's no reason he shouldn't make a complete and full recovery and get back to a normal working day.'

'Provided, that is, that he can be prevented from taking on too much, too soon.' Kenneth was firm.

'Providing he also makes no return to those ludicrous hours of his — positively inviting a coronary. I told him so.' Josh added. 'But in my opinion his angina is stable — though I want him up in London next month to angioscope him. I want to look at the blood vessel surfaces and assess. . .'

The talk about George's condition resumed full spate, and among other things, Gina saw that everyone seemed to be taking it for granted that Ross was going to be with them, in Northborough, keeping an eye on George with the rest of them, and taking most of the load off him, too. So did this mean Ross was going to be staying in general practice after all?

Joy came flooding back, and Gina put her hand towards her glass, drink to this glittering future that unexpectedly was shining so brilliantly ahead. However, she thought better of it. Her glass was half empty again, somehow, and they were still only on the smoked trout.

Opposite her, Ross's dark eyes sparked with inner laughter, and he gave an infinitesimal, admonitory shake of his head, hardly apparent, yet clear as daylight to her. How dared he? She glared back at him, raised her glass to her lips, and took a deep draught. To her astonishment, he raised his own glass — but of course he would have to be drinking Perrier, wouldn't he? — and, she was certain, though how she knew she wouldn't have been able to explain, pledged her across the table.

And across the table she sent her own pledge back to him.

Thankfully no one seemed to have noticed. But perhaps Ross hadn't, either. Perhaps it had only happened inside her own head.

No. It was for real, and they both knew it. She looked across at him again, he gave her another infinitesimal nod, and smiled briefly.

No one had ever smiled at her like that before. Surreptitiously she smiled back, looked into those dark eyes, and knew she had come home for ever.

The waiters began removing plates, there was desultory conversation between neighbours. She was sitting next to Kenneth — she had assumed this mark of distinction to be because, in spite of her junior status, she was the only woman in the party, but now he took her breath away by enquiring casually if she would be at all interested in a session as his clinical assistant at St Mark's?

'Would I be interested?' she breathed. 'You bet I would.'

'It would be for the Wednesday morning outpatient clinic,' he told her.

'Wednesday is my day off, so I'd have no problems about being free them. I'd love to do it, if you'd have me.'

'You did very well this afternoon,' he told her. 'And I gather that besides working on the professorial medical unit at Mortimer's you had a couple of years as cardiology registrar.'

'It was rotating, actually,' she answered honestly. 'Between cardiology and chests. I was the sort of extra body.'

'Good enough. George said you were fretting a bit in general practice, missing the challenge of Mortimer's, and the companionship.'

'Oh, he didn't!' She was appalled. So much for radiating happiness and content at being in general practice in Northborough. 'Anyway, it's not true. I'm truly enjoying general practice, I like following people into their homes. But he's right in one respect — I have been missing the challenge of working alongside my seniors, getting stirred up. Put on my mettle. Doing a morning's cardiology in your clinic would make my week.'

'Not much slips by your father, you know. Well, shall we regard that as settled, then? I'll give you a ring about the mundane details — the present bloke is due to finish at the end of the month, so from the first Wednesday in June, OK?'

'Very much OK. Perfect. Thank you very much.'

'Of course, there's one snag, but I dare say I'll learn to live with it.' He looked at her with an unmistakable twinkle, so she knew it was all right. This was some sort of leg-pull, now she was in. 'My clinical assistants have tended to come from the Central always, but I expect I'll manage to adjust to your Mortimer's ways.'

'More likely educate me out of them. Dad's always trying to do that.'

'I expect to have my mind broadened.'

'Or I will. All this Central influence — I'll soon start taking on local colour.' She smiled at him, and, while he wasn't as bowled over as Ross had been, he certainly thought it would be very pleasant to see this in Outpatients every Wednesday. 'This duck is truly delicious,' Gina was telling him diplomatically.

'Thought you'd enjoy it. They're very good at it here.'

Ross, she saw, was having venison. She'd almost chosen that herself, and now she wished she had. However, the duck was indeed very good, and she surely wasn't so demented that she wanted only to eat exactly the same as Ross forever and ever.

She sighed. That indeed was exactly what she did want.

'How are you feeling now, Ross?' That was Josh, bawling down the table regardless of anyone else, as usual. 'Afraid we gave you a bit of a pasting, eh? Hope you're not too much the worse for wear?'

So she'd been right all the time. Oh, my poor, poor darling.

'A bit tired, sir. Feel as if I've been on a twenty-mile hike. As I pretty nearly have, I must have done about that on your rotten treadmill. Otherwise I'm fine.'

'Good. I've been having a chat with Ken here about your results, and he agrees with me, the trick is going to be for you to familiarise yourself with your limitations, learn to pace yourself and get your feet up before you have any overt symptoms.'

'Josh and I have looked at the tracings,' Kenneth added. 'And our opinion is that provided you go at it slowly and methodically you should continue to improve your performance levels. You'd be very welcome, if you feel it would help you, to come in and use our treadmill, keep on checking yourself in that way. You're bound to learn, like that, more about exactly where your limits are, what triggers the onset of hypotension, how to anticipate trouble. I'll gladly look at your results and have a word from time to time.'

'That's extremely good of you. I'd like to take you up on it, if I may.'

'Do that, Ross.'

'But as for this post with International Pharmaceuticals, now,' Josh boomed down the table again. 'There I'm bound to warn you you'd be a mite foolish to turn it down.'

'It seems to me ——'

'Don't think I don't understand how you feel about it. I never supposed you'd welcome it, and I can't see myself it's much of an advance on clinical management at the Central — except for the money on offer, that is — and we all know you'd didn't go much for that.'

Ross was looking distinctly embarrassed, and Gina felt for him. It couldn't be easy, sitting here while Josh Stirling bawled at him.

'All I can say today,' the voice yelled across the plates, 'is that with careful management — and I do mean careful — your health should stand up to the demands of a full-time post with regular hours and no prolonged standing. Always provided you keep yourself in good condition, keep on exercising, and don't over-extend yourself. But there can be no doubt that over the years a job with a drug firm would be considerably less testing than general practice.'

'However, I ——'

'You'll need to husband your resources in a way you never needed to before that nasty accident.' Sir Joshua talked Ross down, as was his habit. 'In general practice this will be hard to do. I know you have every intention of being sensible and looking after your general health, but it's easy to say, as we sit comfortably here over this meal—good claret, too, Ken, first class—but wait until it's February, you're in the middle of a flu epidemic, you're late on your rounds, you haven't eaten, you've missed out on your exercises and resting with your feet up. I know you—I know any conscientious GP, for that matter—you'd be off to see the next patient and blow what you should be doing for yourself. After all, how did you get this wonky spine, eh? Dashing down the motorway to a multiple crash, and going on to operate when you were warned you were in grave danger, eh? What?'

Gina felt as if she had been thumped between the shoulder blades. Why hadn't Ross *said*?

'In general practice, if you go on like that, you'll soon find out you're not as robust as you thought you were, and then you'd be liable to regret not taking up the drug firm post.'

'I'm very grateful——'

At this point Tom, at the far end of the table, at last succeeded in making himself heard. It was, he said, already a quarter to nine, and Sir Joshua had to be taken to the station for the London train at five past.

'I'll drive you,' James said. 'It's on my way. I'll go straight on to Northborough, look in on George, see how he's weathered the day and settle him for the night. Ross can drive you, Gina—you two can take your time.' He smiled benignly at them, and set off with Josh, still bellowing his thanks backwards on his way to the door.

Half an hour later, Gina found herself sitting along-side Ross in the Volvo. They were alone together. She had so much to say to him — but where to begin?

Ross had no hesitation. 'Great about your Wednesday mornings in cardiology,' he commented, turning out of the car park.

Disappointment flooded her. She didn't want to talk about cardiology. She wanted to talk about Ross, about his accident — a multiple pile-up and he'd been *warned* it was dangerous — and its aftermath, and about what he was going to do about the drug firm post.

'Yes, it should be very interesting,' she agreed neutrally.

He was puzzled. 'I thought you'd be over the moon.'

She must be, mustn't she? 'I am,' she said hastily. 'Of course I am. It's terrific.' But it didn't feel terrific. She was too worried about Ross for anything else to matter. She was in conflict about him. All she wanted was for him to stay in Northborough so that they could be together. But ought he to do this? Was he going to be able to stand up to general practice? Like Josh, she had to doubt it. And she couldn't bear him to try and then fail. But she didn't want him to have to accept this post with the drug firm, when he so obviously hated the prospect. The possibility that he might be forced, for the rest of his life, to devote himself to a job he loathed was so painful that she didn't dare put it into words. In any case, Ross was going to discuss it with Leo Rosenstein at the Central, Josh had said, so there was no reason for her to try and put her oar in. Especially as she could find nothing encouraging to say. She must shut up.

Instead she heard herself blurt out emotionally, 'If

only you needn't take that awful post with the drug firm. Everything else comes second to that.'

They were joining the motorway, he was watching the traffic, his expression remote. She didn't know if he'd even heard her. Perhaps it would be just as well if he hadn't.

She watched the angle of his head, his hands on the wheel, his broad shoulders so near her own. She felt useless. She would have given her entire career to be able to solve just one of his problems, yet she could do nothing. Nothing whatever.

He slid the Volvo into the fast lane, and remarked coolly that his affairs would probably sort themselves out, one way or another, quite satisfactorily.

He wouldn't discuss it. It was like a slap in the face. When it came to something serious, like his health and his future career, he shut her out. Yet for her, any future without him was a desert. What mattered most of all, though, was Ross himself. What happened to him. How he made out. Whether he could manage to defeat this disability that had so unfairly hit him and stopped him in his tracks.

No good telling him so, though. No way could she turn to him and announce that his health and well-being meant more to her than anything in the world. He'd resent it, she knew. Ross liked to think he could look after himself, and he hated anyone to be sorry for him.

Suddenly he chuckled. 'Shall we go through the lanes?' he enquired, and she saw that they were approaching the outskirts of Northborough. His dark eyes glinted sideways, challenging her. He was mocking her again.

'If you like.' She was curt.

He grinned happily. 'Maybe we'd better go round

the conventional way—I'm a less adventurous driver than you.'

She would have been delighted to have throttled him. All this loving and yearning, all this aching to cherish him, to make him well, and he simply sat there making fun of that awful afternoon they'd first met. When she had, face it, behaved atrociously. And what was more, she still owed him an apology for that. No time like the present—and it might at least wipe that grin off his face.

'I'm sorry about that afternoon.' She spoke precisely, in her clear, teaching round voice. 'I behaved very badly indeed, and you were absolutely entitled to be angry. I deserved everything you said.' There. She'd done him proud. She slid her eyes cautiously sideways to check the result.

She had wiped the grin off his face. Good.

'You are quite a dangerous driver, you know,' he remarked.

She took a deep breath, and opened her mouth.

And shut it again. Took another deep breath. 'You're not going to get a rise out of me,' she announced, her chin up.

'Well, it was worth a try.'

He was grinning again. She turned her head this time and looked straight at him. What she saw threw her. He looked young and happy. He must have looked like this, she thought, as a young registrar before his accident. Before she knew him. Her heart lurched.

The Volvo swung sideways, and gravel spattered under the wheels. They were turning up the Rose Bank drive.

'Care to come and have that coffee we missed out on?' she asked impulsively.

She'd startled him, and he shot her an uncertain glance. But then he grinned again, raised his brows above those dark eyes that, yet again, were laughing at her. 'Why not?' he enquired.

One side of her tried to reply snappishly, Don't put yourself out, will you? I wouldn't dream of keeping you if you've anything better to do. However, before these phrases could escape, a quite other side came out with something that startled them both. 'Tell you what,' she heard herself say, 'stop now, at the garage, and we'll go up to my flat. We needn't disturb them in the house.'

Ross looked astonished, but drew up neatly beside the garage, undid his seatbelt, and got out of the Volvo.

The automatic light came on over the garage, and Gina paused at the door to the side entrance, sorting out her keys, her mind racing. What could she be doing?

She hadn't the faintest idea. All she knew was that this lean, exhausted man standing alongside her in his striped and gleaming shirt, his Central tie and his expensive suiting held her heart forever. For better or worse.

CHAPTER ELEVEN

GINA led the way upstairs and into a big L-shaped room. 'Make yourself comfortable,' she said, 'while I lay on the coffee.' She disappeared into the adjoining kitchen.

Ross looked about him. This was his first sight of Gina's own home — would there be anything in it to help him to understand her better?

At first it hardly seemed likely. Daphne's hand was as evident here as in Rose Bank. The same yellow walls, the same large squashy armchairs and sofa, into which he sank with relief — he would have liked, in fact, to stretch out full length, but if he did he'd probably drop off to sleep instantly. And that would be a wasted opportunity, if ever there was one.

Stay awake. Concentrate on the room and on trying to interpret Gina. Primose-yellow bookshelves held a mixture of textbooks, paperbacks and children's classics, and he wondered briefly which of them she took to read in bed — and answered himself promptly. One of the textbooks.

Mingled here and there with the Rose Bank style, he began to realise, was something different. In the wide casement window overlooking the garden stood an untidy desk of black ash, a Breuer chair in front of it. The long coffee-table by the sofa had chrome legs and was topped with smoked glass, though it carried the usual clutter of a busy doctor's life — telephone, answering machine, notepad, a pile of journals. This week's *Lancet* and *BMJ*, and current issues of *The*

Practitioner, *Pulse*, *The British Heart Journal* and *Thorax*, plus, he was intrigued to see, *Vogue* and *What Car?* Attached inelegantly to one of the chrome legs by a loop of frayed string was a cheap and battered ballpoint.

Perhaps he was learning something.

Gina came back with a teak tray holding two pottery mugs, a jug of milk and a bowl of brown sugar, and set it down on the smoked glass.

'Help yourself,' she said shortly. She found herself, to her dismay, without anything to say. He didn't want to talk about himself or his health, and if she wasn't to do that, her mind was blank.

He was exhausted. She'd seen that for herself hours ago. So why hadn't she let him drop her off and go straight back to his own flat and his bed?

Because she'd been unable to part with him. Had she wanted to take him into her own bed? She caught her breath. Wouldn't it be perfect? To lie here in her own bed with him alongside her, to make love, and to hold each other afterwards, tenderly, lovingly, all night long.

But he was worn out. This was no moment to plan to make love all night.

While this battle went on in mind and body, her well-trained other self, the competent registrar, seemed to be talking quite sanely to Ross about cardiology and the proposed Wednesday sessions with Kenneth at St Mark's.

Ross drank his coffee, said yes and no, I should think so, quite, but his dark eyes watched her until she could stand it no longer, and her cover-talk dried up.

'That's better,' he said affably. 'Take a breather.'

'A — a breather?' Oh, no. Obviously she must have been boring him out of his mind.

'You've been edgy ever since we came in. I don't bite, after all.' What was the matter with her? She wasn't usually like this.

They weren't usually in her flat, of course. And then he understood. That was the trouble. She'd invited him in — and it had been a surprise. So perhaps he'd over-reacted, she'd picked it up — she was never, ever slow on the uptake — and now she was afraid he'd put the wrong interpretation on what had been no more than a casual invitation. A throwback to her Mortimer's days, a relaxed gesture after a day's work. But now she was panicking, because she was afraid he'd misconstrued her offer, and she didn't know how to get rid of him.

True, he had wondered, and undoubtedly there was nothing he'd like more than to seize her and make love to her, here and now, on this sofa where he was sitting. But not unless she wanted it as much as he did. 'No need to panic,' he said lightly. 'I'm not the brutal and licentious soldiery, remember. I'm not going to rape you.' He grinned reassuringly.

She took a deep breath, and he expected to be demolished with all the Mortimer's clout she could so easily summon. Not for the first time, she was to surprise him.

'I'm sorry,' she said. 'I'm being difficult and — and silly, I can see. It's just that. . .' Her voice dwindled. She wasn't going to be able to come out with it. She'd intended to be honest, to say, 'Yes, I'm panicking, but it isn't because I'm afraid you'll rape me. If you'd just grab hold of me I'd love it. But you won't let me anywhere near you, and I can't bear it.' But she couldn't say it. It wouldn't come out. So she said, weakly, the first thing that came into her head. A half-truth. 'You're always laughing at me,' she told him grumpily. She sounded, she realised despairingly, like a cross seven-year-old. 'What's so funny about me, anyway?'

'Nothing, love,' he told her tenderly. She was over-tired, that was what was wrong. Worn out after the afternoon and evening at St Mark's. 'You're tired,' his voice caressed her. 'Time I went. It's been a long day for both of us.' They were both tired, come to that. And tomorrow would be another day. What's more, there were going to be all the days they needed ahead of them, too. He leant forward, picked up his mug, drained his coffee. 'Thanks for the coffee.' He stood up, patted her on her shoulder, planted a chaste kiss on her cheek, and walked across to the door. 'I'll let myself out,' he said. 'You hit the hay.'

Gina sat in the armchair opposite the sofa where he'd been. She heard the door downstairs slam behind him. She heard his footsteps on the gravel, the thud of the Volvo's door, the engine starting up. She listened to the hiss of gravel, and then the sound receded down the drive. Silence. She put a hand, wonderingly, up to her cheek where he'd kissed her.

Eventually she took the coffee-tray into the kitchen, rinsed the mugs, left them upended on the draining-board, let herself out of the flat, and walked across to Rose Bank.

She fell asleep instantly, which was not what she expected, and was woken by her alarm. As she show-ered and cleaned her teeth, she discovered that she knew precisely what she was going to do.

When she reached the surgery, she asked Betty if Ross was down yet.

'In his room,' Betty said. 'He's asked for his first patient. I was just ——'

'Hold it a moment, will you? I want to have a quick word with him.'

She knocked and went straight in. 'As you are no doubt about to point out,' she said belligerently, 'I am not exactly your first patient.'

'Quite so.' The black eyes glinted at her.

He was laughing at her again. But she wasn't going to react, she was going straight ahead with what she'd come to say. 'I came to ask you,' she said clearly, very clipped and professorial medical unit, 'if you'd care to come for a meal in the flat tomorrow evening?'

For a split second his jaw dropped, she was delighted to see. This was not what he'd been expecting her to say. Good. She'd surprised him.

He made a rapid recovery, though.

'Thank you.' He was smoothness itself, not so much a hint of surprise apparent. 'I'd like that very much.'

'Great. I'll look forward to it.' She turned on her well-shod heel, and his door clicked shut behind her.

She ran into problems, though, with her mother when she mentioned over supper that she was having Ross to a meal the following evening.

'Oh, lovely, darling.' Daphne beamed. 'Won't that be nice? Now, what shall we give him to eat?'

Feeling rather as if she were stealing candy from a toddler, Gina steeled herself and said firmly, 'Sorry, Ma. I mean I'm having him to a meal in the flat, if you don't mind. I——'

'But Ross is a friend of us all.'

George intervened. 'We can see him one by one, though,' he pointed out pacifyingly. 'You and I can have a quiet evening together, eh?'

'I would quite like to do my own entertaining in my own home still,' Gina said. 'You don't really mind, do you?'

'No, darling, of course not. What do you want to eat? There's that new recipe for chicken breasts — shall I do that for you?'

'I can cook, you know, Ma. Not as well as you, but I can do a bit more than boil an egg.'

'Of course, darling.' It was Daphne's turn to be indulgent. 'But you're so rushed. Are you absolutely sure you wouldn't like me to do you a nice casserole in the slow cooker? I could make it here and plug it in over in your kitchen, all ready for you when you come in?'

It seemed unkind to go on refusing. 'Well,' Gina began. 'If you're —'

Daphne waited for no more. 'I can try out something from one of the new books,' she said eagerly. 'Chicken breasts in yoghurt and mint, say? Or there's another with them in orange and almonds. Just choose, and I'll see to the rest.'

Gina gave in. The orange and almonds sounded great, she assured her mother, and fled across to her own flat to flick a duster and tidy up. It looked bleak and impersonal, she thought. Some flowers?

Nonsense. All Ross was going to be thinking about was getting her into bed as fast as possible. It was all she was going to be thinking about, too. She'd given him a green light, she'd meant it, and neither of them were going to care what the place looked like.

So what was she doing, planning the great seduction scene with soft lights, wine and flowers? Neither of them would be thinking about anything except each other.

She wanted it to look like somewhere nice to come home to.

Grow up, Gina Hurst. Ross isn't expecting a little woman in a frilly apron, the reliable home-maker.

He's planning on an evening's sex. Be your age, woman.

Friday was particularly busy, and it slid hectically by. Gina snatched a few extra minutes to rush back to the flat in the lunch hour with cream for the raspberries she had in the freezer — which she now took out. The slow cooker, duly plugged in, was emitting an enticing aroma of orange and spices, there was a bottle of her father's claret ready on the countertop, and the salad drawer was stuffed with washed lettuce. Smoked salmon to start? She took that out of the freezer, too, and dashed out to the garden to pick a few tulips.

Arranging them, she ate an apple and a few chunks of cheese, drank a mug of Nescafé, decided to cook rice to go with the chicken. She could do that this evening, and make a salad, and change into something more seductive than her pleated skirt and walking shoes.

But what?

Her black suit with the emerald chiffon top? No, right over the top. She'd just do her face, change into another shirt, and wear her plain courts. That would have to do — and would probably be all there'd be time for, in any case.

Surgery that evening was busy, and when the last patient went, she heaved a sigh of relief. She was through. Only her notes to write up, and she could make for home.

She should, of course, have known better than to allow any such thought to cross her mind. The telephone rang. Betty. 'Gina, I've got Mrs Oliver on the line. That's right, *Mrs*. Not Miss. She says she's worried about her daughter, who's collapsed.'

'I'll go and see, Betty. Mrs Oliver has never rung before, has she? No. There must be something really wrong. Tell her I'm coming straight over.' Frowning, she shrugged her coat on, picked up her bag, and went out into the hall. 'Tell Ross where I've gone, would you, Betty? And say I'll give him a ring as soon as I'm through.'

Miss Oliver lay back in an easy chair opposite the telephone, breathing stertorously, and unresponsive to anything going on. Gina checked her airway, looked at her pupils, felt her pulse and her forehead, listened to her chest, and worried away in her mind about what she was going to do about Mrs Oliver, who was clearly going to be left on her own. Miss Oliver would have to be admitted to hospital at once.

'Did your daughter complain at all about feeling unwell?' she asked, continuing her examination of the patient.

Mrs Oliver, a spare upright figure, still charming in a fluffy mohair cardigan that matched the faded blue of her eyes and set off her short flyaway white hair, shook her head. 'She was perfectly all right until it happened,' she said. 'Of course, she always did get excited about nothing, and she was very excited tonight over the TV. I've turned it off now, but I wish I had earlier — that's what it was, I'm sure. Well, it was a silly interview, two uppity young things in the most peculiar garments laying down the law about how the world should be. And she got upset, poor dear, and started shouting at them. As if it would make any difference, as I often told her. And then she stopped, and gave a sort of snort, her voice got all thick, and the next thing I knew she was lying back like that. There didn't seem to be anything useful I could do for her, so I rang you. Thank you for coming so quickly. I was worried. She's had a stroke, do you think, Doctor?'

'I'm afraid that's what it looks like. We'll have to get her into hospital.'

'Oh, dear. I've been thinking about it, but I don't really see how I can possibly look after her properly. But she'd want to stay here with me, I know.'

'No, you can't look after her yourself, Mrs Oliver. I'll get her into hospital.' And then you into a nursing home, Gina thought to herself.

'She'll be so frightened without me — she's never been anywhere on her own, you see. I should have tried harder, I know, made her do things on her own — never mind, too late now. But I wish I had persevered. It won't have to be too far away, Doctor, will it? I'd like to be able to go in and sit with her during the day, at any rate.' The blue eyes might be faded, but they were alert and intelligent — and, at present, Gina realised, not in any way frightened. Perturbed, and caring, yes, but not panicking.

'She has to have nursing care, Mrs Oliver — but suppose I get her into the cottage hospital to begin with? Just for a day or two, while we see how she goes along, and look round for somewhere more permanent. How would that be?' And if necessary Mrs Oliver could go into Vicky's too, Gina was thinking. They weren't full at present, and there was no pressure on the beds.

'Oh, Doctor, that would relieve my mind. Any of my neighbours could drive me in and out, and it wouldn't upset their day too much. I was afraid you were going to say she'd have to go to Halchester, and that's such a very long drive.'

Evidently Mrs Oliver was prepared to stay on at home on her own, Gina saw. Well, she'd play it by ear, see what transpired. 'Can I use your telephone?'

'Of course. In the hall, Doctor.'

Gina spoke to Abby, who'd just come on duty and then rang the ambulance service.

'That's all arranged,' she told Mrs Oliver, who was sitting on a low stool beside her daughter, holding her hand, chafing it, and talking softly to her as though to an invalid child. 'Now, what about you? Are you going to be able to manage on your own, or would you like me — ?'

'Oh, don't worry about me, Doctor. I shall be perfectly all right.'

Gina remained uneasy about this, but as soon as the ambulance drew up at the house hordes of worried neighbours from either side and from opposite, and then from further along the road materialised and took over, and she was able to drive back to Vicky's behind the ambulance without anxiety.

Abby and one of the auxiliaries were waiting for the patient, with a bed ready.

'I'm sorry, Abby,' Gina said. 'This is going to be a trial for you, but I hadn't the heart to send her straight off to St Mark's, even if I could have persuaded them to find a bed. Her ninety-five-year-old mother is so very anxious to come and sit with her that I found myself promising we'd take her in here for a few days, anyway.'

'No problem.' Abby, as ever, was cheerful. 'I don't see how you could have done anything else.' She looked thoughtfully at the patient, whose condition was unchanged. 'Amazing, though. Ninety-five, you say? And it looks as if she'll see this one out.'

'She's a tough old bird, always has been — and her daughter the exact opposite. I should have realised that sooner.'

'There's a message from Ross, by the way. He was over here earlier, and I told him you were arranging

for Miss Oliver to come in, so he said give him a ring
if you'd like him to admit the patient for you.'

Gina was tempted, but shook her head decisively.
'No need for him to do that,' she said briskly. 'All
perfectly straightforward—I reckon you and I can
manage unaided, don't you?'

'Of course,' Abby agreed. 'In that case, he said to
tell you, he'd be in his flat when you want him.'

'Right. Thanks, Abby. Now, let's see. . .' She began
a second and more detailed examination of Miss
Oliver—whose name, she had ascertained from her
mother, was Marion, though she didn't answer to it,
nor did she respond in any other way when spoken to,
shouted at, or touched.

'Quite an extensive bleed, I'm afraid,' Gina commented. 'Still, maybe given time she'll improve a bit.
But I'm not exactly hopeful.'

'No,' Abby agreed. 'She doesn't strike me as one of
those where it wears off, given time. Let's hope I'm
wrong—it's no more than a feeling, an instinct.'

'Well, let's do what we can.'

They worked together for what, occupied as they
were, didn't seem particularly long, and Gina was
shattered when, ready to leave, she glanced at her
watch. Ten o'clock, would you believe? So much for
her lovely evening with Ross. 'I'll just ring through to
Mrs Oliver, and then I'm off,' she told Abby. 'Don't
hesitate to ring if you want me—I'll see Ross first, so
I'll be opposite to start with, and then later on the
home number as usual.'

Mrs Oliver's telephone was answered by an alert
and cheerful young voice, who turned out to be the
teenage daughter of a neighbour. 'I'm staying here for
the night,' it informed Gina. 'So that I can answer the
telphone, like now, and get my parents to drive Mrs

Oliver to the hospital if necessry. Do you want her to come in?'

'No, I was going to tell her not to think of it until tomorrow.'

'I'll tell her, shall I? We persuaded her to go to bed about half an hour ago—she was exhausted, though she wouldn't admit it. I'm afraid she doesn't have a telephone by her bed.'

'Tell her her daughter's stable, and quite comfortable. We don't feel there's likely to be any change tonight, but if there is we'll let her know. You say your parents are ready to drive her if necessary?'

'That's right. It's why I'm here, really—we were sure she'd hesitate to call us out in the night, she'd be trying to ring for a taxi instead. But we'll drive her in absolutely at any hour.'

'Tell her, then, we'll surely ring if we feel she should come in, but it's really not very likely. I'll ring her in the morning after breakfast to tell her how things stand. All right?'

'Fine,' the voice said brightly. 'Marion's stable and quite comfortable, and you'll ring in the morning after breakfast. Right?'

'Spot on. I leave it to you, then—hope you have a good night's sleep, and we don't have to disturb you. With any luck we shan't. Goodnight.'

Gina went in search of Abby, and told her the state of play. 'The neighbour's daughter'll answer the telephone, if you do have to summon her, and they're standing by to drive her straight in,' she said. 'So you don't have to worry about waking a ninety-five-year-old and giving her alarming news. The neighbours will cope.'

'That helps,' Abby agreed. 'However, as it's all laid on so nicely, I reckon we shan't need to call her out.'

'How right you are. Well, this time I'm really off. Have a good night, and I hope we don't meet again before the morning—I'll be over then. Night.'

Ross opened his door with a mug of coffee in his hand, and an enquiring expression on the lean face that she loved so inescapably. 'All through?' he asked. 'Or is this just a short break?'

'Through for now. I'm dreadfully sorry about the evening. It seems to have disappeared without trace.'

'It's only just after ten. The night is young. I've done my round, you've settled your patient, the rest of the day is ours. You look all in.'

So she looked all in. Thanks, Ross, so very much for your truly flattering words.

He was surveying her still. 'You're worn out,' he informed her. 'How about a coffee before we begin to think about the rest of the evening?'

'I could do with it,' she admitted.

'I'll get it,' he said. 'Make yourself comfortable. You know where everything is in this place, I'm sure.'

'That's right—since I was small. Can I just pop into your bathroom?'

'Go ahead. Coffee coming up.'

Gina crossed the hall to the big old nursery bathroom, turned on the light, and examined her face in the mirror over the basin. A disaster area. So much for all her hopes and plans. No wonder Ross said she looked all-in. She scowled at her reflection. Perhaps a wash would help, make her look more like a normal human being. She ran the taps, splashed cold water on her face, dried it on Ross's towel, and held it briefly, crazily, lovingly, to her cheek, while desolation engulfed her. She'd hoped for so much from this evening, and look at it. Look at her.

She reached for her sling bag, which she'd left

hanging on the bar of Ross's exercise bike, and then stood, transfixed.

The room, filled with Ross's exercise apparatus, was more like a small gymnasium than a bathroom. She ought to have remembered. Betty had said so.

But it was the photographs that had stopped her in her tracks. There were four of them, each neatly labelled in his angular script. The first showed him, laughing, at the tiller of a sailing boat, and read 'Round the Island, 1990'. Less than four years ago, and he looked, she saw with anguish, ten years younger and altogether different. Oh, Ross, my darling Ross, what has life done to you?

The second photograph had him flat on his back in a hospital bed, surrounded by gadgetry, and read 'Royal Wessex, 1991'. In the third, labelled 'Stoke, 1992', he was in a wheelchair, but in the fourth he was on his feet, with crutches, admittedly, and his legs in callipers. He was wearing a not at all unfamiliar expression of barely concealed triumph, and the caption read 'Central, 1993'.

Gina wanted to cry. Instead, totally forgetting that she'd been going to do her face, she walked across to the sitting-room, where she found him sprawled on the chesterfield. At last, she did what she had been longing to do so often. Put her arms round him and held him tightly. 'I wanted to make this evening so lovely, and it's all gone,' she muttered into his striped shirt. 'And I love you so much.'

He jerked as if he'd been hit, and she was sure he'd turn round and demolish her, but instead he put his own arms round her, and they felt like bands of steel. 'Good,' he told her. 'Thank God for that, because I love you. I have ever since I first saw you.'

'Nonsense,' she said, remembering. 'Don't be idiotic. You loathed me.' Not that it mattered any more.

'Hindsight,' he said. 'But true, none the less.' He kissed her long and thoroughly.

Eventually they came up for air and stared at each other joyously.

'You don't know how long I've been wanting to do that,' he said.

'Me, too.'

Her eyes held the deep green glow Ross had ached for, while his were fathomless pools of love for her to drown in for ever, she knew. She traced the line of his brows and touched his cheeks with hands inexplicably trembling.

His arms went round her again, her bones seemed to melt, and time ceased to have any meaning. After what seemed like hours — or, alternatively, no time at all — he murmured into her hair, 'What are we doing here? We'd be much more comfortable in the other room.'

'So we would,' she agreed.

Somehow they found their way, still glued together, along the hall and into the bedroom, and fell on to the bed. And then everything Gina had yearned for was for real. They made love — wild, ecstatic love — and fell asleep in one another's arms.

She woke to find Ross leaning on his elbow and staring down at her from those dark eyes brimming, now, with tenderness. 'I've never seen you sleeping before.'

She smiled radiantly. 'You'll get used to it, I dare say.' Her mouth quirked.

He kissed her at once. 'Do that at me,' he said, 'and this is what you'll get. You know we never actually had that coffee? I was just going to make some more and bring it to you.'

'Super idea. What's the time?' She stretched languorously.

'Just after one. We've the entire night ahead of us.' And now his eyes held the familiar glint.

The difference was that now she loved it.

'Coffee'd be great.' She thought fleetingly of the casserole in her kitchen, but forgot it again as he kissed her.

Somehow, though, she must have passed a picture to him, because he asked, 'Are you starving? When did you last eat?' The dark eyes glinted again. 'Very important to keep your strength up, after all.' He kissed her gently on the lips, pushed her hair away from her face with lingering fingers.

'Don't know. Doesn't matter.'

'Can't have that. I can offer you muesli, but that's about all, I'm afraid.'

'You know,' she sat up and regarded him seriously, 'black coffee and muesli does seem immensely attractive.'

'Right. Back shortly.'

She watched his departing back with love and despair. His legs were long and scarred, and outlines of surgical repair showed clearly around his spine, so that she wanted to reach out and hold him safely for ever.

He returned with a tray he put down on the side of the bed, then reached for a pullover lying on a chair and draped it round her shoulders. They ate muesli together, and drank coffee.

'To be here, close to you like this is all I want out of life,' she said mildly surprised. 'I feel—it's quite mad, of course, but I feel as if nothing can ever go wrong again.

'Absolute certainty.' His eyes looked straight into her soul in that extraordinary way they had. 'To be honest, I've never, ever felt like this before. As if we were destined for each other, and now that we're together, that's it. Complete at last. As the old song has it, now that I've found you, I'll never let you go. So there.' He raised his coffee mug to her. 'To you. Forever.'

'How I'm ever going to bear to let you out of my sight, I don't know.' Her eyes glowed green with a light that reached a depth in him that no one had touched before. 'I just want to stay close to you and never stir,' she told him. 'And here we are, with two flats — help, and one of them with supper still cooking.'

'Never mind, we can have it for breakfast.' He was unperturbed. 'I dare say we'll be hungry again by then and in need of a substantial meal.'

'Our new life, starting with a new sort of breakfast. Smoked salmon, chicken casserole, and raspberries. Don't expect me to keep that up for the next twenty years.' Her own eyes were glinting now.

'You know what that is?' he demanded at once. 'It's a wedding breakfast, that's what it is. We'll eat it this morning, and then in the weeks ahead we can fit in the tedious formalities of the actual wedding and the required paperwork.'

'Would you by any chance be proposing to me? Because if you are, fair warning, I shan't let you get out of it.'

'I am proposing, and I have no intention whatever of getting out of it. Gina Hurst, will you marry me? To have and to hold, from this day forward?'

'I will.'

'And thereto I plight thee my troth.' He kissed her.

This was, they both agreed later, the end of the beginning.

MILLS & BOON

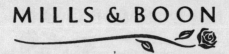

HEARTS OF FIRE by Miranda Lee

Welcome to our compelling family saga set in the glamorous world of opal dealing in Australia. Laden with dark secrets, forbidden desires and scandalous discoveries, **Hearts of Fire** unfolds over a series of 6 books, but each book also features a passionate romance with a happy ending and can be read independently.

Book 1: SEDUCTION & SACRIFICE
Published: April 1994   *FREE* with Book 2

WATCH OUT for special promotions!

Lenore had loved Zachary Marsden secretly for years. Loyal, handsome and protective, Zachary was the perfect husband. Only Zachary would never leave his wife…would he?

Book 2: DESIRE & DECEPTION
Published: April 1994   Price £2.50

Jade had a name for Kyle Armstrong: *Mr Cool.* He was the new marketing manager at Whitmore Opals—the job *she* coveted. However, the more she tried to hate this usurper, the more she found him attractive…

Book 3: PASSION & THE PAST
Published: May 1994   Price £2.50

Melanie was intensely attracted to Royce Grantham—which shocked her! She'd been so sure after the tragic end of her marriage that she would never feel for any man again. How strong was her resolve not to repeat past mistakes?

MILLS & BOON

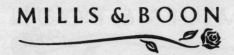

HEARTS OF FIRE by Miranda Lee

Book 4: FANTASIES & THE FUTURE
Published: June 1994   Price £2.50

The man who came to mow the lawns was more stunning than any of Ava's fantasies, though she realised that Vincent Morelli thought she was just another rich, lonely housewife looking for excitement! But, Ava knew that her narrow, boring existence was gone forever...

Book 5: SCANDALS & SECRETS
Published: July 1994   Price £2.50

Celeste Campbell had lived on her hatred of Byron Whitmore for twenty years. Revenge was sweet...until news reached her that Byron was considering remarriage. Suddenly she found she could no longer deny all those long-buried feelings for him...

Book 6: MARRIAGE & MIRACLES
Published: August 1994   Price £2.50

Gemma's relationship with Nathan was in tatters, but her love for him remained intact—she was going to win him back! Gemma knew that Nathan's terrible past had turned his heart to stone, and she was asking for a miracle. But it was possible that one could happen, wasn't it?

Don't miss all six books!

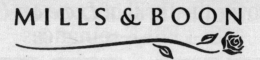

MILLS & BOON

Discover the thrill of *Love on Call*
with 4 FREE romances

FREE
BOOKS FOR YOU

In the exciting world of modern medicine, the emotions of true love acquire an added poignancy. Now you can experience these gripping stories of passion and pain, heartbreak and happiness - with Mills & Boon absolutely FREE! AND look forward to a regular supply of *Love on Call* delivered direct to your door.

❧ ❧ ❧

Turn the page for details of how to claim 4 FREE books AND 2 FREE gifts!

An irresistible offer from Mills & Boon

Here's a very special offer from Mills & Boon for you to become a regular reader of *Love on Call*. And we'd like to welcome you with 4 books, a cuddly teddy bear and a special mystery gift - absolutely FREE and without obligation!

Then, every month look forward to receiving 4 brand new *Love on Call* romances delivered direct to your door for only £1.80 each. Postage and packing is FREE! Plus a FREE Newsletter featuring authors, competitions, special offers and lots more...

This invitation comes with no strings attached. You may cancel or suspend your subscription at any time and still keep your FREE books and gifts.

It's so easy. Send no money now but simply complete the coupon below and return it today to:

Mills & Boon Reader Service, FREEPOST, PO Box 236, Croydon, Surrey CR9 9EL.

- - - - - - - - - ✂ `NO STAMP NEEDED` - - - - - - - - - ✂

YES! Please rush me 4 FREE *Love on Call* romances and 2 FREE gifts! Please also reserve me a Reader Service subscription. If I decide to subscribe, I can look forward to receiving 4 brand new *Love on Call* romances for only £7.20 every month - postage and packing FREE. If I choose not to subscribe, I shall write to you within 10 days and still keep the FREE books and gifts. I may cancel or suspend my subscription at any time simply be writing to you. I am over 18 years of age.   Please write in BLOCK CAPITALS

Ms/Mrs/Miss/Mr _____ EP62D

Address _____

_____

_____ Postcode _____

Signature _____

Offer closes 30th September 1994. The right is reserved to refuse an application and change the terms of this offer. One application per household. Offer not valid to current Love on Call subscribers. Offer valid only in UK and Eire. Overseas readers please write for details. Southern Africa write to IBS, Private Bag, X3010, Randburg, 2125, South Africa. You may be mailed with offers from other reputable companies as a result of this application. Please tick box if you would prefer not to receive such offers. ☐